The reviews are in for

The Long Escape

"'I am a native of San Francisco. I still like San Francisco better than any place except possibly Guatemala City....' These words appear on the dust jacket of Traitor Dodge's new book. For shame, Davy, for shame. Nevertheless, the new book is a honey. Al Colby, Mexico City's favorite private-eye, follows the mysterious trail of one Robert R. Parker from Pasadena to Santiago, Chile. It's all very colorful and very exciting."

~Edward Dermot Doyle, *San Francisco Chronicle*

"A neat puzzle, considerably enhanced by an authentic-sounding South American background."

~*New Yorker*

"Romance, shooting and even a bit of grave-robbing."

~*The New York Times Book Review*

"Plenty of punch and color....Better grade."

~*The Saturday Review of Literature*

"Mr. Dodge, an experienced baffler, is now working his way through Latin America with considerable effect....With its peppering of local color, scraps of Spanish and transportation details, this sounds a bit like a travel tome entitled 'So You're Going to Antofagasta;' that is, until the plot begins to boil in that old cemetery. Lively writing,"

~Will Cuppy, *New York Herald Tribune Weekly Book Review*

"Dazzling scenery and some equally dazzling doings en route."

~*Christmas Book Issue (San Francisco Chronicle)*

Books by David Dodge

Novels
Death and Taxes
Shear the Black Sheep
Bullets for the Bridegroom
It Ain't Hay
The Long Escape
Plunder of the Sun
The Red Tassel
To Catch a Thief
The Lights of Skaro
Angel's Ransom
Loo Loo's Legacy
Carambola
Hooligan
Troubleshooter
The Last Match

Travel Books
How Green Was My Father
How Lost Was My Weekend
The Crazy Glasspecker
20,000 Leagues Behind the 8-Ball
The Poor Man's Guide to Europe
Time Out for Turkey
The Rich Man's Guide to the Riviera
The Poor Man's Guide to the Orient
Fly Down, Drive Mexico

This edition of *The Long Escape* is a tribute
to the DELL "Mapback" mysteries
published in the 1940s and 1950s,
which are a delight to collect and read.

THE LONG ESCAPE

DAVID DODGE

Introduction by
Randal S. Brandt

To Dawn—
Thanks for your hospitality
to MWA NorCal!
Enjoy! *Randal Brandt*

Bruin Books   **The Emerald Empire**   **Eugene, Oregon**

Published by
Bruin Books, LLC
December 2011

Introduction Randal S. Brandt 2011

Title page photograph © 2008 by Gerhard Hüdepohl
The photo was taken in August 2008 in the town of Baquedano, Chile,
about 60 km northeast of Antofagasta. The location is an old abandoned
railway station, a relic from the glory days of Chile's nitrate mining boom.

This book was edited by Jonathan Eeds
Graphics design by Michelle Policicchio

Special thanks to:
Kendal Lukrich and Randal Brandt

Printed in the United States of America

ISBN 978-09826339-8-4

Bruin Books, LLC
Eugene, Oregon, USA

Visit the scene of the crime at www.bruinbookstore.com

For more information on David Dodge
visit www.**david-dodge**.com

Gerhard Hüdepohl's photography can be found at
www.atacamaphoto.com

THE LONG ESCAPE

David and Elva Dodge, with Kendal, circa 1946

David Dodge's Long Escape

David Dodge, full-time tax man, part-time mystery author, and self-confessed "nickel-nurser" and "skin-flint," did not act without a sound financial plan. Thus, it might have seemed out of character when, in 1945, Dodge, freshly released from active duty by the U.S. Navy, packed his wife Elva and 5-year-old daughter Kendal into a car and trekked over 3,000 arduous miles south from San Francisco for an extended stay in Guatemala just for the fun of it. No doubt, before making this journey, Dodge had performed the necessary monetary calculations, but this rationality may have been cloaking more bohemian aspirations.

Dodge's youth was marked by a tension between fiscal responsibilities and adventurous yearnings. Just weeks before his ninth birthday, his father was killed in a car accident, leaving him the sole male in a household made up of his mother and three sisters. By the age of sixteen, after the family had moved from Berkeley to Southern California, Dodge had dropped out of high school and taken a job as a bank messenger. He advanced his career in the financial industry by enrolling in night school classes at the American Institute of Banking and eventually moved up to the position of supervising the bank's commercial books. Yet, in 1931, he succumbed to the siren call of adventure by quitting the bank to become a marine fireman on a South American run for the Grace Steamship Company. This was Dodge's first chance to see the world outside of California and, even though his time at sea was relatively brief, it clearly made a deep and lasting impression (and not only as represented by the self-applied propeller tattoo on his left arm). In 1933, he came ashore to work as a stevedore and waterfront night watchman in San Francisco, but by 1934 he had returned to the financial industry, going to work for the San Francisco accounting firm of McLaren, Goode & Co. He became a Certified Public Accountant in 1937, not long after his 1936 marriage to Elva Keith, and published his first mystery novel in 1941.

Dodge's dual careers in accountancy and mystery writing continued through the World War II years. While working as an accountant in the Office of Supervisory Cost Inspector, 12th Naval District in San Francisco, he was also turning out novels featuring San Francisco tax expert and reluctant detective James "Whit" Whitney. The tone of his four Whitney novels— *Death and Taxes* (1941), *Shear the Black Sheep* (1942), *Bullets for the Bridegroom* (1944), and *It Ain't Hay* (1946)—gradually darkened, as shown by the evolution from *Thin Man*-esque banter between Whit and his love-interest Kitty MacLeod (later Whitney) to Whit's internally-voiced fear that Kitty will justifiably run off to Mexico for a quickie divorce. At this point, a reader of Dodge's fiction might have been able to predict that just as the fictional Whit and Kitty seemed poised for life-altering changes, so might be their creator.

When David, Elva, and appealingly precocious Kendal took off for Central America they left family and friends behind who wanted to hear about the progress and exploits of the travelers. In 1949, *Ellery Queen's Mystery Magazine* described the situation: "Dodge started writing a letter to his friends in the States, telling all about the first leg of their trip, through Mexico and Guatemala. The letter got so voluminous that Dodge concluded it would be more economical to publish it as a book, and send out copies, than to mail carbons to all and sundry by air. Thus, his best-selling travel story, *How Green Was My Father*." In fact, between the publication of his last Whitney novel, *It Ain't Hay*, in 1946 and the appearance of *The Long Escape* in 1948, Dodge transformed himself into a travel writer. Two popular, humorous "sort of travel diaries" called *How Green Was My Father* and *How Lost Was My Weekend* were published in 1947 and 1948 and chronicled the trip through Mexico to Guatemala and the two years spent living in Guatemala City.

In *How Lost Was My Weekend*, Dodge provides one explanation of why his family pulled up roots and drove to Central America:

We went to Guatemala to get a fresh outlook on the business of murder. I had shot, strangled, stabbed, poisoned and otherwise knocked off so many people *in the vicinity of San Francisco that the well was running dry. Unless I could find a fresh crop of victims, the time was fast approaching when I would have to give up writing murder mysteries and take a job in a shoe store to earn a living. This fate worse than death was precluded when one of my wife's distant relatives left her with a small inheritance. Together with our lifetime savings of $172.50, it gave us enough of a bankroll to follow the swallows south to Central America.*

His assertion that he had to leave San Francisco because "the well was running dry" of plots is a little hard to believe. That particular well is very, very deep, as evidenced by the ongoing flow of new mysteries set in the area. A more likely story is that the confluence of circumstances—his release from the Navy, his increaseing success as a writer, the inheritance, and the age of his daughter—enabled him to finally resume scratching the travel itch.

The effect of Dodge's newly-acquired expatriate status on his fiction was immediately apparent. The first leg of their journey took the Dodges south, via the Pan American Highway, to Mexico and Guatemala on a route not unlike the one that his new sleuth Al Colby, an American expatriate private investigator based in Mexico City, follows in the opening chapters of *The Long Escape*. After two years in Guatemala, the family continued south to Peru, where a large part of the action in *Plunder of the Sun* (1949) takes place. Further travels around South America resulted in the third Colby adventure, *The Red Tassel* (1950), set in Bolivia.

From then on, Dodge alternated between writing fiction and travel literature. He penned light-hearted travel memoirs, best-selling travel guides such as *The Poor Man's Guide to Europe* (a Book-of-the-Month Club selection that was revised and re-issued each year from 1953 to 1959), and numerous magazine articles throughout the rest of his life. These popular works paid many Dodge family bills. In addition, living abroad continually filled his metaphorical well for locales and characters to populate his novels, including the glitteringly popular *To Catch a Thief* (1952), written while the Dodges were living in the South of France. Looked at in this way, Dodge's seemingly impractical and romantic notion to uproot his family and set off for exotic lands turned out to be a savvy economic choice indeed.

© Randal S. Brandt
Berkeley, California
October 11, 2011
www.david-dodge.com

This is for
DON GUSTAVO STAHL
of Guatemala

1

IT STARTED out like any other job. I was in Mexico City, getting ready to drive down to Cuernavaca for a weekend with friends who had a house there, when the letter reached me. It came registered air mail, so I took it along for the weekend instead of sticking it in a drawer until Monday.

When I got around to opening it, the envelope held a fuzzy snapshot of a middle-aged Joe Doakes squinting into the sun, a photostat of an Examining Physician's Report on an insurance company form, another photostat of a note addressed to Dear Helen, and a long letter from a lawyer I knew in Los Angeles named Adams. Adams' letter said:

Dear Al:
Here is a chance for you to earn an honest penny.

Robert R. (for nothing, as far as I have been able to learn) Parker disappeared from Pasadena, California, five years and some months ago, leaving behind him a wife, no children and substantial valuable real estate. All the other information I have been able to assemble about him is contained in the enclosed documents.

Parker appears to have been something of a man of mystery. He was married for fifteen years to the same wife and spent his entire married life in Southern California, yet neither his wife nor his friends know anything definite about his early life; i.e., where he came from, or where he got his stake, or what the score was in any respect. He is said to have stated that he was born in San Francisco. I can find no record of him there. You may be aware that all San Francisco birth records were destroyed in the 1906 fire, a convenient fact for anybody who is old enough and who requires a native birthplace to keep from being deported or for other reasons. Of course many people *were* born in San Francisco prior to 1906. He may or may not be one of them.

On the surface, Parker seems to have been just another man who parlayed a modest sum of money into a respectable fortune on the increase in Southern California land values. This is the reason for my interest in him. Knowing your ignorance of legal matters, I will simply state in words of one syllable that much of the real property which he acquired during his married life qualifies as community property under California law, and a wife cannot transfer clear title to community property while her husband is living, unless he joins in the transfer. Inasmuch as the wife, my client, has been offered approximately a quarter of a million dollars for clear title to a piece of said community property, I am very anxious either to get in touch with Mr. Parker or to obtain sound evidence that he has departed this vale of tears. Personally I would prefer to learn that he is dead, as this would simplify matters, but I do not suggest that you take any steps to help him from this life to a better one.

For your further information, I will state confidentially that my client, the wife, is a first-class bitch, and I do not blame Parker for running out on her. How he stood it for fifteen years is more than I can understand, after a rather brief business relationship with her. I inject this apparently irrelevant note as a possible explanation for her complete lack of any information about her husband's background, as she spends so much time talking about herself that she probably never listened to anything he had to say. On the other hand, it seems strange that she would not have learned a few things about him during the course of fifteen years of marriage, unless he was being careful that she should not, and it occurs to me that he may have had something to conceal; e.g., a criminal record or some such thing. This is only conjecture on my part, of course, but it might explain why he was so shy about being photographed. I have been able to discover only the one poor snapshot which is enclosed.

Parker's last note to his wife, a copy of which is also enclosed, was mailed from Mexico City, which is the reason I am turning the job over to you. Please do your utmost to get a line on him. If he is dead, send me a death certificate or its equivalent, plus whatever affidavits you can obtain from people familiar with the circumstances of his death. If he is alive, persuade him to get in touch with me. You can promise that no attempt will be made to interfere with his personal life, as Mrs. P., who is considerably younger than her husband, has plenty of other boyfriends and refers to Mr. Parker as "that old bastard." Her only interest is in the money. I think she might also enjoy making him squirm if there were any way she could do so—she seems to resent the fact that he left her before she could leave him—but as far as I know he has committed no offense worse than simple desertion, which is not a crime in this state when you leave the desertee as well-fixed as she will be *if* she gets the money from the sale of the properties. Note the "if," which will be an important arguing point in case he is non-cooperative. You can promise him the moon if he will sign the necessary papers. His note to her, copy enclosed, clearly shows his intent to relinquish interest in the properties but does not constitute sufficient evidence of the relinquishment for our purposes. It will be approximately another two years before we can have him declared legally dead, and the two hundred and fifty thousand dollars will not wait that long.

It may be of help to you to know that Parker left here in a brand-new (five years ago) Buick sedan, California license 5C-71-25, engine number 2032245, serial number 6JA11-4548. I have been unable to trace this car, and I think he may have driven it into Mexico. At least it is an angle to work on.

I have persuaded my client to guarantee expenses and a reasonable fee for your services up to a maximum of $2500 *in toto*. I will add unofficially that if you deliver the goods, a small bonus may be in order as well. Please give me action, as time is of the essence.

Regards and best wishes. How is your golf?

Chuck.

I didn't feel much like working just then, but a chance at twenty-five hundred dollars is always interesting. I looked over the rest of the stuff that had come in the envelope.

The snapshot wouldn't be any help. Parker had a hat on, and either because of the sun or because he knew what he was doing, he had screwed his face up until you couldn't tell whether he looked like Clark Gable or Jo Jo the trained chimp. His physical condition, according to the insurance company report, was so-so for a man of thirty-five, which he had been when the examination was made. No scars or other peculiar marks of identification. He had a lot of fillings in his teeth, according to a chart that accompanied the medical report. I worked the dates around to make him fifty when he pulled his freight from Pasadena and fifty-five or fifty-six when I started looking for him.

The "Dear Helen" note told me that he had a conscience. All it told Dear Helen was that Robert was taking a powder for reasons which she would understand without his going into unpleasant detail, that he was going where she would be unable to trace him, that all the property was hers to do with as she saw fit, and that she could obtain a divorce or not as she liked, goodbye. Most men who run out on a wife after fifteen years either leave a long alibi pinned to the pillow, because they are in the wrong and know it, or simply duck blindly out of a bad situation and the hell with farewell letters. My guess was that Parker had been in the second class. But in the time it had taken him to get from California to Mexico City, his sense of duty had eaten at him until he had to tell Dear Helen what was what, so there would be no tag ends. Otherwise he was a chump to have written at all.

The brand-new Buick was my biggest help. I figured he would have to sell it if he really wanted to drop out of sight. You need an export permit to sell a United States car in Mexico unless you have owned it for six months. The U.S. consul will give you an export permit if your story is good.

I went down to the consulate. A fellow I knew there nosed through a bunch of old records and came up with the information that an export permit for one new Buick had been issued to Mr. Robert R. Parker on the day before the date on the "Dear Helen" note. My man didn't know the details of the transaction.

It took me a while to run the Buick down. It would have been a hopeless task before the war, when everybody in Mexico City bought a new car every year and the old ones turned into *libres*, which ended up on the junk-heap after about six months in the hands of the average *libre* jockey. But not many new cars had come into Mexico for a long time, so the Buick was still doing business. I found it registered in the name of Señora Molly Jean Mendoza.

Señora Molly Jean Mendoza lived in a pretty good apartment house out toward Lomas de Chapultepec. A frowsy maid let me in without asking my name or business, then went to call the *señora* while I parked my hat on a pile of American movie magazines.

Molly Jean turned out to be a *rubia,* a brassy blonde of the type a lot of Mexicans go nuts about. She was any age you want to guess, with a sulky mouth. She greeted strange gentlemen visitors in a form-fitting housecoat with a zipper running from neck to hem in front that practically said Pull me, kid. The handle of the zipper was a little bell that tinkled when she walked.

I gave her a card I had had printed a couple of years before, when I was on a job for an insurance company. It had the company's seal on it, my name down in one corner, and "special representative" in the other corner. She thought I was an insurance salesman. Before she could dust me off, I said, "I won't take much of your time, Mrs. Mendoza. My company is interested in a man named Robert R. Parker, who sold a Buick here in Mexico City five years ago. I understand that the car is now registered in your name."

"Is it?"

Just like that, she was going to give me information for nothing. In a pig's eye.

I said, "My company is offering a reward of two hundred and fifty pesos for information."

That was more like it. She said, "Sit down. Have a cigarette."

We sat down and had a cigarette.

"Is the car hot?" she asked, with girlish innocence.

"Not that I know of. I'm just interested in Parker."

"What do you want to know about him?"

"Whatever you know."

"I don't know anything about him. My husband—my

ex-husband—bought the car for me. I never laid eyes on the guy."

"Perhaps your ex-husband could tell me. . . "

"My ex-husband wouldn't tell you the time." She stuck out her lower lip, pink inside, darker outside where she had slapped on fresh lipstick over the old after the maid told her that a *señor* was calling. "Anyway, why should I send you to him with two hundred and fifty pesos?"

"No reason. Could you get the information from him for me?"

"I can try."

She stood up and tinkled over to the telephone, giving me a play with her rear end. I said, "Ask him where he met Parker, and if he has any idea where Parker was going, if he was going anywhere, or if he ever heard of him again, and what else does he know?"

"Leave it to me, sweetheart."

Molly Jean dialed a number on the phone.

She dialed the number three more times before she got a connection, because that's the way Mexican telephone systems work, and each time she said something different about Mexico and the Mexicans generally, nothing favorable. She must have been a great little help to her husband during their marriage. I guess he thought so, too, because when she finally got him on the line he said something that, from the rattle of the receiver, was more or less an invitation for her to go drown herself and stop bothering him.

She said, "Oh shut up," and switched over to Spanish

with a Muscatoon, Iowa, accent, giving me a quick peek out of the corner of her eye. "Did you know that Buick was stolen when you bought it?"

I looked at my fingernails.

He said something loud and short. She said, "What Buick do you think I mean? The one you bought from the American. A detective is here looking for him."

He said something else, not so loud and not so short. She said, "It doesn't matter to me if you spend the rest of your life in jail, but I want to keep the car. Tell me all you know about Parker and I'll see if I can . . ."

He talked for five minutes. When he ran out of words, she put her hand over the receiver.

"He says he met Parker at the bar in the Hotel Reforma. He doesn't know where he came from or where he was going, or anything else about him. He bought the car because Parker was anxious to sell it and gave him a good price, but he didn't know—he didn't think there was anything wrong, because Parker had the ownership certificate and a passport to prove his identity. My husband gave him a check and got a bill of sale. It was all on the level."

There wasn't anything else I wanted to ask. Anybody who could dream up a stolen car as fast as she had could probably dream up answers for me regardless of what her ex-husband told her. I said, "Thanks."

She hung up the phone, without saying goodbye, and tinkled back to her chair. I took two hundred and fifty pesos out of my wallet and held the bills in my hand.

"I'd like your ex-husband's full name and address,

please."

She didn't want to give it to me, but I was still holding the money. After she had written the address for me on a card, I said, "You haven't supplied me with much information, Mrs. Mendoza. I'd like to pay you the reward, but I don't feel that I can conscientiously do it—yet. Is there anything else—anything at all—that you can tell me which might help me to find Mr. Parker?"

She looked at the money in my hand like a fish squaring off at a worm.

"I don't know. I don't think—wait a minute."

She tinkled into her bedroom. I heard her slamming drawers around. Then she yelled for the maid. Pretty soon she came back and handed me a little photograph, not much more than passport-photo size.

"They found it under the front cushion in the Buick when I had the seat covers changed. I don't know who it is or what it means, but you can have it if you want it."

It was a picture of a little boy, seven or eight years old, a good-looking kid with his hair slicked down, big eyes, and a solemn expression. There wasn't anything to indicate where it had been taken or when or by whom, except that the kid's clothes looked old-fashioned and the paper on which the print had been made was that brownish stuff most photographers gave up using years ago. It had the flat scuffed look that a piece of paper gets when you carry it in a wallet or a notebook for a long time.

It wasn't worth two hundred and fifty pesos, but I gave Molly Jean the money. She tucked it down behind the little bell at the top of her zipper. She already bulged the housecoat enough so that there wasn't much room for the wad of bills, but she made it.

"Thanks," she said. "Any time I can do something else for you, let me know. I'm in the telephone book. Any time."

I said, Sure, I'd let her know, and picked up my hat.

She went to the door to let me out, hipping along ahead of me so I could see there was plenty she could do for me any time I was really interested. I never heard a bell tinkle afterward without seeing that tart's behind bouncing down the hall.

2

MOLLY JEAN'S ex-husband, whom I went to see that afternoon, was about what his taste in women would lead you to expect. He was an importer, with an office on Avenida Madero. I didn't let him know that the Buick wasn't really hot until after we had finished talking, because I figured he'd tell me all he knew if he thought he was in trouble. But he didn't know anything more than what I had already learned.

Parker, whom he had met over a highball, had asked him if he knew of an English-speaking car dealer. Parker's Spanish had been pretty weak for business. Mendoza spoke English and was in the market for a car himself. They had made a deal. The price had been a little too good, from Mendoza's viewpoint, so he had been careful to compare Parker's passport and owner-ship certificate.

I said, "What kind of a passport was he carrying?"

Mendoza looked blank. I said, "What nationality?"

"United States."

"Did he look like this picture?"

Mendoza studied the fuzzy snapshot and then spread his hands.

"Anyone could look like that picture. He looked like

any other—*estadounidense.*"

He had been going to say *gringo,* but changed it because he didn't know how I would take it. I said, "He didn't speak Spanish?"

"He spoke Spanish, yes. But it was poor. Not like a *turista,* you understand. More as if he had known the language well at one time and had forgotten it."

That was interesting. I asked more questions about Parker's Spanish, but Mendoza had told me all he knew. When I saw that the well was dry, I eased his mind about the Buick and went home to think things over.

I had made a little progress. I knew that Parker held a United States passport. It meant that he hadn't made his break on the spur of the moment, because you don't get a passport overnight. It also meant, probably, that he did not intend to stay in Mexico. You only need a tourist card to get into Mexico, and you can get a tourist card in five minutes at any consular office for a couple of dollars. The fact that he had sold his car also pointed in the direction of further travels. A car is a handy thing to have when you are buzzing around the States on good roads, but south of Mexico City the good roads are few and far between.

O.K., I said. Mr. Parker is just passing through. Where is he going?

I couldn't answer that one.

O.K., then. What else do you know about him?

He speaks rusty Spanish.

That could mean something, some time, but not yet. What else have you got?

A small boy's photograph.

I thought about the photograph for a long time. I didn't believe that Molly Jean had made up the story about finding it under the seat cushion, because I knew she could have done better for two hundred and fifty pesos if she had wanted to try. But even assuming that the picture belonged to Parker, and that it had slipped out of his wallet while he was showing his papers to any one of the eighty-four people who would want to look at them between the Texas border and Mexico City, it was strictly zero evidence. He hadn't left any kids behind in Pasadena. The picture could be a nephew, friend, brother, his old man, a bastard son of his youth, himself, or something he had won in a bingo game.

The passport angle was all I really had to work on. I went back to the consulate on the off chance that they might know something.

They didn't know much, but they had more on Parker than they would have had if he hadn't had to get the export permit. He was traveling on a passport restricted to the Western Hemisphere, which was the way most passports were issued in the years after the war.

That made things real easy. Writing off Canada and the States as improbables, I could expect to find Parker in (a) Mexico, (b) one of nineteen other American republics, (c) Belice, (d) the Guianas, (e) the Caribbean islands, or (f) at the South Pole. I left Iceland off the list. I knew it was technically part of the Western Hemisphere because I spent a couple of years there with an Army rifle guarding a lot of ice after the destroyers-for-bases deal, but I figured Parker wouldn't go to Iceland by way of Mexico City unless he was as dopey as the War Department, who made me list all of my qualifications for service in Latin America, including a better Spanish vocabulary than an English one and good contacts all the way from Nuevo Laredo to Punta Arenas, and then sent me to Reykjavik. I didn't think Parker was that dopey.

There are times when you have to do things the hard way. I took my hat in hand and went around to the consulates. Wherever I knew somebody I asked for information, and wherever I didn't know anybody I paid *mordida*. Adams would scream like an eagle when he saw *mordida* on my expense account, but it's the easiest way to do business in Mexico City. And it didn't cost him much. I got a strike at my seventh consulate.

Parker had obtained a visa for Guatemala. This surprised me, because Guatemala was right next door. If he was planning to hide out there, he was leaving a pretty broad trail.

It was a cinch that he had gone on by plane. The Pan American highway still had a big gap in it north of the Guatemalan border, steamer services from Acapulco and Vera Cruz were catch-as-catch-can, and nobody in his right mind would ride the narrow gauge railway that stumbles down the Isthmus of Tehuantepec whenever the tracks haven't been stolen. I hopped the first flight out for Guatemala City.

What I had in mind was a nice, quiet five-hour session with the plane's magazine rack. I didn't get it. An old boy with a limp grabbed the seat next to me, introduced himself as Doctor somebody or other, and bent my ear from the middle of Mexico to the middle of Guatemala. Inside of half an hour I knew everything that he did. He was going to Guatemala for his arthritis, he had three children and four grandchildren, he liked old-fashioneds made with Southern Comfort, he was an Elk, he had performed the first successful osculecto-mistotomy on the Pacific Coast, and so on. I couldn't brush him off for just being friendly. When we sat down at Guatemala City, I was worn to a frazzle.

Doctor Gimp was staying at the Hotel Victoria. He wanted me to be sure to look him up there and have a Southern Comfort old-fashioned. I said I'd be sure to do that. When he finally unhooked himself and went away, I hunted up a fellow named Jaime, a friend of mine who worked at the airport.

Jaime was checking over the flight list of the plane I had come in on. I said, "What's the name of the doctor who sat next to me on the plane? An old bird, traveling alone."

Jaime ran his finger down the flight list.

"Only one doctor aboard. A. R. Benson, U. S. citizen. Widower, age sixty-five, weight eighty kilos, destination Guatemala, passport number 1605, profession retired, three pieces of luggage. Want me to find out where he's staying?"

"I already know where he's staying. I just want to look out for him next time I take one of your planes. Do you have the same vital statistics on all of your passengers?"

"Sure."

"See what you can give me on Robert R. Parker. He landed here about five years ago, maybe a few months over."

"Five years ago? Are you kidding?"

"No. I'm on a job, Jimmy. I'll pay for the research, if you have a man you can put to work on it."

Jaime was a good boy. I had to wait around until his shift was finished, but then he took me into town and we spent half an hour in a file room leafing through old flight records until we found Robert R. Parker coming in.

All I learned that I didn't know already was that his weight had held pretty steady during the fifteen years since he had taken the physical examination for the insurance company. His destination, according to the record, was Guatemala, which didn't mean a thing. He was carrying one piece of luggage, which didn't mean a thing either, except that he was traveling light and fast.

I said, "On a hunch, let's see if we can check him out again. My guess is that he didn't stay more than a week or two."

He had stayed six days. We dug up another flight record that booked Robert R. Parker on to Tegucigalpa, in Honduras.

My first idea was to go right on to Tegoose and pick up the trail there. But I had time to think about it, since I couldn't get a plane until the next day, and I began to get curious. Why had Parker spent six days in Guatemala? I knew it wasn't to admire the scenery.

There are only three or four good hotels in Guatemala City. I checked them. My man had stayed at the San Carlos, as I learned for the five *quetzales* it cost me to get the clerk to let me nose through old registration cards. I had Parker's dates down cold by then, and I knew his handwriting from the Dear Helen note, or I would have missed it completely. He had signed himself Roberto Ruíz P.

This will look like a joke to a lot of North Americans, but it made me sit down and readjust my sights. In Latin America, a man uses both his father's name and his mother's name as his own. The son of Joe Blow and Mary Doe, for instance, is legally Joe Blow Doe. In the South American countries, he is sometimes addressed as Señor Blow Doe and sometimes as Señor Blow, but in Central America he is usually Señor Blow, although he may sign his checks Joe Blow, Joe Blow Doe, or Joe Blow D. My man, as long as he had to use his passport, was still Robert R. Parker. But he could also get by as Robert Ruíz Parker, Roberto Ruíz P., and, for all practical purposes, Roberto Ruíz.

I sweated gumdrops figuring this one out.

I had started with a middle-aged *estadounidense* who didn't speak enough Spanish to be able to sell an automobile in Mexico City. Now I had a man who was using a Latin name, who knew enough, half an hour after landing in Guatemala, to sign himself as a Central American would, and whose Spanish was picking up fast. The last part wasn't just a guess. He *had* to speak

Spanish if he was going to be Roberto Ruíz. As far as appearance went, he could be anything, because there isn't any more of a standard Latin American type than there is a standard North American type. Half my friends were redheads or sandy-colored people named Guillermo Ramirez Cruikshank or Juan Wurdemann Ayalá or Andrés Martínez Levy. Roberto Ruíz Parker would fit in anywhere.

I didn't have any luck tracing him around Guatemala. He had stayed two nights at the San Carlos, checked out, checked back in again three days later, and left for Honduras the next morning. I followed him.

Smelling out a five-year-old trail in the States would be impossible. People move around too freely. In Central America, you have to have visas and exit permits and clearances with the National Police and Ministries of the Interior and Ministries of War, Navy and Aviation and customs officials and immigration officials and health authorities and a few others. I had them all, as well as good connections, so traveling for me was just normally difficult. Robert R. P., who had started from scratch, left a trail like a snowplow.

He was Robert R. Parker at Toncontín airport in Tegucigalpa, because that was what his passport said. He turned into Roberto Ruíz at the only good hotel which had been operating when he was there, and he was still Roberto Ruíz when he booked passage to La Ceiba, on the Caribbean coast, by way of SAHSA, the jerkwater airline that carries coastal traffic. He didn't need a passport for that jump.

La Ceiba is a banana port; hot, steamy and dirty. It squats and swelters at the shore end of a pier where ships tie up to load bananas brought down from the plantations on a narrow-gauge railway. The town offers an open-air movie when you get tired of watching the banana trains, and a casino with a marimba band when you get tired of the movie. That's the works. The only sensible reason for going to La Ceiba would be because you were a banana on your way to the States, or because you wanted a job with the fruit company. Parker wasn't a banana.

I went to the fruit company offices, told them my business, and asked for a peek at their employment records. They were a lot more obliging than I had a right to expect. I was turned over to a girl who brought out a raft of books and helped me dig.

She was a nice kid, about twenty. We didn't find anything in the books, but I took her to the casino that night. We drank fresh pineapple juice and I listened to her talk English with the funniest accent you ever heard. She had been born in Utila, one of the Bay Islands that lie thirty miles off the Honduranean coast, and her English had come down from the British pirates, Sir Henry Morgan and Blackbeard and the others, whose crews had intermarried with the natives. Her own name was Morgan.

She said, "My mudder wahs from Belice. My great-great-grahnd-fadder wahs an Englishmon, a piraht. I ahm a Hondurahnean. Isn't thaht funny?"

"Have you ever been to the States?"

"Oh, no, mon. But wahns I went to Tegucigalpa, and I hahv been in Tela ahnd Puerto Cortes many times."

Tela and Puerto Cortes were other banana ports up the coast a couple of hours by boat. I said, "You must know this part of the country pretty well."

"Yes, mon."

"Maybe you can tell me something. What would make a man, an American who did not need a job and had no interest in bananas, want to come here to La Ceiba?"

I didn't mean it quite the way it sounds. She thought La Ceiba was some punkins, after the islands, and she got huffy. I smoothed her down and asked the same question in a different way.

She said, "Perhaps he wanted to go to the States. The bahnahnah boats carry pahssengers."

"Could he get clearance papers here—visas and things like that?"

"I don't know, truly, mon. Mr. Henderson could tell you thaht."

"Who is Mr. Henderson?"

"He works in our accounting department. He is ahcting United States sub-consul here."

"I'll talk to him tomorrow. Let's dahnce—dance, I mean."

She introduced me to Mr. Henderson the next morning.

He was a dried-up, precise-mannered old piece of leather who had been with the company for forty years. His acting sub-consul's job was a sideline that paid him a little gravy for fixing up the papers of anybody who wanted to ride the banana boats. I asked him if he knew anything about a man named Roberto Ruíz or Robert Ruíz Parker or Robert R. Parker, who might have wanted something from the United States acting sub-consul five years before.

He recognized the name. I knew it by the way his eyes flickered. It struck me as strange, because you wouldn't expect a name to ring the bell right away after five years. And he began to sweat, which was even stranger. It was hot enough down here on that tropical coast to make my shirt stick to my back and my underwear feel like melted fly paper, but I had been living in the highlands for so long that I couldn't take the lowland heat. The pirate's great-great-granddaughter, who had brought me to Henderson's office, looked pleasantly cool. So did everybody else I had seen, except Henderson.

He said, "Parker? Why—I can't say. I'd have to look at my records."

"I'd appreciate it."

He went to get them.

I had an idea I'd be able to dig more out of him if there was nobody listening in, so I told the girl she needn't wait and maybe we could have another pineapple juice later in the day. She said, Yes, mon, and went away.

Henderson came back.

"I remember now." He had got over his first scare. He didn't look so moist over the eyebrows, now. "Mr. Parker wanted to know if he could obtain passage on a ship going to the east coast of South America."

"Where did he want to go in particular?"

"We didn't get that far. There are no ships leaving from this part of the country for the south except occasional nitrate carriers returning to Chile. Mr. Parker did not want to go to the west coast."

"All of the company's ships go north?"

"Yes. To the States or to England."

"I see."

I didn't see anything, but I thought about it. Mr. Henderson looked at the floor, at his desk, at the clock, and out the window at the coco palms along the beach.

I said, "Had you ever met Parker, or heard of him, before he came to La Ceiba?"

"No."

"Did you ever meet him again or hear of him, after he left here?"

"No."

"The only time you ever had anything to do with him was during his one visit here?"

"Yes."

"What happened while he was here?"

"I beg your pardon?"

"What happened between you and Robert R. Parker that bothers you now because I am asking questions about him?"

He looked at me. His leathery face got wet all over again. He didn't say a word.

"He didn't have to come to the accounting department to find out about ship schedules, did he?"

He still didn't answer. He just got wetter and more miserable.

It wasn't the kind of digging I enjoyed, but I got it out of him at last. He thought I was FBI or something, and when I talked about calling in the company manager, he gave up. The company manager is God in those little banana ports.

It turned out that he had renewed Parker's passport, probably for a price, although we didn't go into that, and had spent five years worrying about it because he wasn't sure that he had the necessary authority. The passport had been a regular two-year deal, open to a two-year extension which any consul could authorize. But Henderson was only a lousy acting sub-consul, and the poor devil had been expecting the United States Secretary of State down on his neck every day for five years because he had exceeded his authority. No wonder he remembered Parker's name.

He almost cried when I said it was nothing to me what he had done. I told him that the passport had probably gone where nobody would ever see it again, so he needn't worry too much about it. Then I asked him if Parker had spoken English or Spanish.

He thought for a while.

"Both."

"You sure?'

"Yes. He spoke English with me. But we have many Spanish-speaking employees here, and one of them brought him to my office. I remember that he thanked the man for his courtesy."

"You mean '*gracias*'?"

"A little more than that. And I think I must have heard him speak it at other times, because I have a distinct impression that he was bi-lingual. Most of us are here, you know."

"You'd say his Spanish was adequate, then?"

"Yes. Certainly adequate."

"Would you recognize him from this picture?"

Henderson peered nearsightedly at the snapshot.

"I would say it was he if it were shown to me as his picture," he answered cautiously. "I would not pick it out of a group of pictures."

"Can you give me any idea at all of his general appearance?"

Henderson looked old and apologetic. I said, "Was he fat, thin, tall, short, blue-eyed, brown-eyed, dark-skinned, light-skinned? Did he wear glasses? Did he have a mustache? Did he have a wart on his nose? How would you describe him?"

"I—I'm afraid I'm not very observant about such things. He was just an average elderly man with no particular distinguishing characteristics. I'm sorry. I only saw him for a few minutes, and it was a long time ago."

"It doesn't matter. Thanks a lot."

I left Mr. Henderson with his five-year-old guilty conscience and went for a swim.

3

THE GUEST HOUSE that the banana company turned over to me was a clean little cottage down by the beach in a grove of coco palms. The cottage was mostly verandah, screened all around against sand flies and furnished with a refrigerator full of cold pineapple juice. Late that night, after I had gone for another swim—the moon was up, and the surf felt like warm soup—I got myself a milk bottle full of pineapple juice out of the refrigerator and went into conference with it and the Parker documents.

I hadn't gained ground on him. On the other hand, I was learning more about him every day. I didn't know why be had picked a backwater like La Ceiba as the place to get his passport renewed, unless he just happened to notice that it was running out while he was there, but the fact that it needed renewing meant he had held it for two years, so he must have been planning his getaway for a long time—long enough in which to learn how to speak Spanish, for example. But I was pretty sure he hadn't learned his Spanish in the States. The know-how to keep two names and two identities alive within the limitations of a single passport wasn't something he would have picked up in Pasadena, California. He knew Latin America. He also knew where he was going, which I didn't, and he had not overlooked the possibility that some poor sucker like me would try to follow him. I was pretty sure that when I got to where he had made his real jump, both Robert R. Parker and Roberto Ruíz P. were going to dissolve in thin air, leaving me holding the sack. My only chance was to shortcut him, some way.

The trouble was that I didn't have the ghost of an idea how to go about it. I went back and forth over the papers Adams had sent to me like a bird dog working a field for quail. No ideas came to me. I studied the little kid's picture until I could see it with my eyes closed, trying to picture what he would look like at the age of fifty-five. It was a fair bet that the photo was either Parker or a relative who might look like Parker when he grew up, and if I ever caught up with my man I had to know what he looked like. I drew about a million sketches that night, trying to piece together from Parker's snapshot and the kid's picture something I could show to the next person I questioned. When I found myself putting cock eyes and bugle noses on the sketches, I went to bed.

From La Ceiba Parker had gone on to Puerto Barrios, Guatemala's main Atlantic port, in a bouncy cutter that made the run once a week. I hope he was as seasick as I was when I followed him.

In Barrios I talked to a man at the United Fruit Company office and confirmed what Henderson had told me. There were no ships sailing from the east coast of Central America to the east coast of South America. If

Parker really wanted to get there by boat, he would have had to go to New Orleans and book passage from there, or pick up a ship at the Canal Zone.

I said, "How would he do on the Pacific side?"

The fruit-company man wasn't sure.

"I don't know what it was like five years ago. Today, he might catch an empty cabin on one of the Grace freighters at San José. He might not, too. It's hard to say. If you want to come back this afternoon, I can send a wire to Guatemala City . . ."

"Thanks, no. I have to go back that way anyhow."

"How about lunch, then?"

I made a face and told him about the bouncy cutter. He had traveled on it himself, so he knew why I wasn't hungry.

I couldn't trace Parker out of Barrios. But if he had gone to New Orleans he was out of my territory, and if he hadn't gone to New Orleans his next logical move was back to Guatemala City. A plane left for Guatemala City on Tuesdays. This was Thursday, so I went up on the train that left at seven the next morning—eleven hours in a rattle-trap day coach with hard plank seats, clouds of dust coming in through the open windows, warm beer from bottles carried through the aisles by a barefooted *mozo,* and nothing to eat except what you could buy wrapped up in a plantain leaf from the Indian women who swarmed under the train windows at each station. By the time we limped into Guatemala City, I was so pooped and so dirty that I didn't give a damn if Parker had sprouted wings and flown off to Cuba.

I slept for fourteen hours and went back to see Jaime at the airport.

He said, "*Por Dios*, what *is* this guy, anyway—a carrier pigeon?"

"I don't know, but I'm getting as tired of him as you are. How about taking a look through your flight records for a week or so after he went to Tegoose?"

"Did he come back here?"

"I don't know. I want to know if he left here."

"Which way would he be going?"

"South, probably."

We went through the flight records again. Mr. Robert R. Parker had left Guatemala for Balboa, in the Canal Zone. Destination Balboa.

I didn't follow him. I was running out of clean shirts, for one thing, and you need plenty of clean shirts in Panama. Also, I thought I had an idea what he might have been doing during the six days he had spent in Guatemala on his first lap. To check this, I got Jaime to give me a note to a man at the Grace Line office.

It was a lucky break. The Grace man had a good memory, and he had been transferred from Peru to his Guatemala job just five years before. Parker—Ruíz, this time—was practically the first customer he talked to. It had stuck in his mind the way events do on your first day at a new job or a new marriage or in the army.

"I remember him well," he said. "He wanted to buy passage to South America. I didn't know beans about the job then, and the man who had it before me left things in a mess, so I had to dig like a beaver to find out about rates and schedules and bookings. We had a freighter in at San José. I told Ruíz I didn't know whether she could accommodate him or not, but if he wanted to take a chance, I would give him a note to the agent at the port, who knew more than I did, and he could get his information from the horse's mouth. He took the note and went to San José."

The Grace man grinned, shaking his head.

"I don't know what happened after that. I suppose he thought I was just trying to get rid of him."

"Why would he think that?"

"Because all of our vessels on this run go down the west coast. He'd have to transship at the Canal, to get to the east coast. If I'd used my head I could have arranged a passage for him out of Panama and sent him there by plane."

"He wasn't interested in going to the west coast?"

"No. It was east coast or nothing."

That made twice that Parker had shied from the west coast. I put it away to think about later.

"What else can you remember about him? Did he look anything like this picture?"

I showed him the snapshot. He said, "Your guess is as good as mine."

"How about this?"

I tried him with my best sketch. He shook his head. I said, "Well, for Christ's sake, what *did* he look like?"

He was going to snap me up on that. I headed him off.

"I didn't mean to sound tough," I said. "I'm jumpy.

I've been trailing the guy all over Central America, and I haven't yet found anybody who even remembers if he was clean-shaven or wore a ring through his nose. Anything at all you can tell me would help."

The Grace man looked at the ceiling.

"Nope," he said at last. "It's too long ago. I can see his outline, sitting in that chair where you are, but I can't fit in any of the details. He didn't impress me as young, or old, or fat, or thin, or tall, or short, or good looking or ugly. What would you remember about a man you had talked to for a few minutes five years ago?"

"Less than you do. I'm just trying every angle I can think of. Did he speak Spanish?"

"Yes."

It had that half-questioning note that means, "Of course." I said, "Better Spanish than English?"

"He didn't speak English."

The Grace man saw the expression on my face. He said, "Wait a minute, now. I take that back. I mean to say that when a man comes into your office, carries on a long conversation in good Spanish, uses absolutely no English words at all and has to have shipping schedules translated for him, you assume that he does not understand the language in which the shipping schedules are printed—particularly if he has a name like Roberto Ruíz."

He gave it the Guatemala accent, which made it "Shroberto Shruíz." I said, "Did he have that 'Shroberto' accent?"

The Grace man laughed.

"No. That was a joke."

"Do you know accents pretty well?"

"Fairly well."

"Where would you say he learned his Spanish?"

"That's a pretty tough question."

"I know it is. If you can't answer it, forget it. But sometimes a man will leave an impression by the way he mushes his 'r's' or buzzes his 'y's' or swallows his 'd's', so that you automatically think 'Guatemala' or 'Argentina' or 'Colombia.' I know I do. And there are other tip-offs. We say 'bue-no!' in Mexico when we answer the phone. You can tell a Mexican every time if you hear him using a phone. Here in Guatemala you use 'vos' instead of 'tu', as they would say 'che' in Argentina. In Peru they have a word for 'adios' —what is it—like 'che'. . ."

"Chau." The Grace man nodded. "I know what you mean. Let me think."

He looked at the ceiling again for a long time. I crossed my fingers.

"It's only a guess, of course," he said.

"I want anything I can get. Shoot."

"Chile."

"Why?"

"Because he used the word 'roto' to mean a peasant, a poor man—what we call a *descalzado* here in Guatemala. I told him that even if he could get aboard the freighter at San José, the accommodations wouldn't be much to brag about. He said he wasn't particular; anything that would do for any *roto* would do for him. I never heard *roto* used like that by anybody except a Chileno."

"Neither have I. Anything else?"

"I only remember the one word. I'm afraid it isn't much to go on."

"It's better than anything I've got so far."

We talked about shipping for a while. I promised to send him a good box of cigars from Mexico if he could get it through the customhouse. When I was leaving, he said, "It isn't any of my business who this man is or why you are looking for him, but I wonder why he didn't just hop a plane and fly to South America. He was certainly anxious to get there."

He looked at me curiously.

I said, "He probably wanted to Go Grace, savoring the luxurious pleasure of a perfectly appointed floating palace where Courteous Service is the watchword and no expense is spared to insure the passenger's comfort as he sails across romantic tropical seas to where the Southern Cross hangs like a glowing beacon in the sky. Am I getting the publicity right?"

The Grace man laughed and said I was pretty close. I thanked him for his help, put on my hat, and took the afternoon plane back to Mexico City.

One of the plane's motors got an attack of heartburn near Tapachula. We spent a stinking night there. Tapachula is a hot little hell-hole on the coastal plain just over the border inside Chiapas. We hit it right in the middle of a *temporal,* one of those soggy, steaming rains that dribble on without a break for days. My hotel room was so muggy I couldn't sleep. I sat up naked most of the night writing a report to Adams, the sweat dripping off the points of my elbows and making puddles on the floor while the rain dripped down outside and made puddles in the mud.

First I put down all I had learned. Then I put down what I guessed, which was to the effect that Robert R. Parker, the wealthy Pasadenan, was either in reality a Latin American or had spent so much time in Latin America that he could pass himself off as a Latin American, if he wanted to, when he got to where he was going. I didn't know where that was, but I offered the guess that he was heading for Chile. This I based on what the Grace man had told me, plus the fact that, although Roberto had been hot for a ship, any ship, which would take him to the east coast of South America, he had shown no interest at all in the west coast. It is only four or five hours by air from Valparaíso to Buenos Aires, and I knew he wasn't afraid of airplanes. It seemed logical that he was being careful not to leave a trail to the west coast because the west coast was where he intended to end up.

It looked pretty convincing when I had it all written down. I went on with a few more shots in the dark.

Parker had found that he couldn't lose his identity as long as he kept his passport. He had brushed up his rusty Spanish until he could pass as Roberto Ruíz, but he was Parker on the passport and needed the passport to get around. This was the real answer to the Grace man's question which I had answered with the wisecrack about Going Grace. There is no way you can hide your trail if you travel by plane. Too many people are around to note down in nice neat handwriting just how much you weigh and what the name is on your papers and where you got on and where you got off and what time it was and how many pieces of baggage you were carrying. A ship is different. But Parker hadn't been able to get a ship from Central America so he had gone on to Panama. There he could either buy himself a set of phony papers—it isn't as hard as you'd think—or, failing that, get a bunch of visas on his passport for every country south of the Canal and then book ship passage to some place like Buenos Aires. At Rio or Santos or Montevideo or some other place where he *could* buy a set of phony papers, he and the ship would part company. Nobody would know where he got off. And nobody would ever hear of Parker again, or Ruíz, either. Somebody named Pancho Chancho would turn up in Chile later.

This was how it looked to me from that sweaty hotel in Tapachula. I didn't know why Parker was going to such pains to muddy the waters behind him, but I suggested to Adams that his client must be even more of a bitch than he had said. It would take a woman with two heads, both covered with snakes, to make me work as hard as Parker had worked to get away from her.

The report was pretty long before I finished with it. It still wasn't much to give Adams for the thousand dollars it had cost. I explained that I had not gone any further with the job because the next step was either to try to trail Parker out of Panama or go to Chile and sniff around there. Either step would run the cost well over his $2500 maximum. I recommended that he turn the job over to somebody who could work from the Chile end, thanked him for the business, and told him my golf was as bad as ever.

When I got back to Mexico City I mailed the report and my bill off together with all the stuff he had sent me. I added a P.S. at the last minute. It said:

I am also sending along a small photograph which was allegedly found in Parker's Buick and for which I paid fifty dollars. The fifty dollars is included in the enclosed bill, so the photograph is your client's property.

If Parker's wife and his friends do not recognize it, it probably has nothing to do with him, but it is my only tangible contribution to your case and I send it along for what it is worth. It should at least serve to remind you that, since Parker carried a passport, the State Department will have a copy of his passport photograph. However bad such a picture may be, it will look a lot more like him than the lousy snapshot you sent me. I suggest that you try to get a copy of the picture before proceeding further.

I honestly thought I was through with Mr. Parker when I put the report in the mail.

4

SIX DAYS LATER the job bounced right back in my face.

Adams' letter was shorter and hotter than his first one. It started off with, What was the matter with me, couldn't I read English? He had asked me to find Parker, not tell him how to go about it. The expense limit was now $5000 *in toto,* and a check for my fee and expenses to date was enclosed, together with the stuff I had sent back to him. With a quarter of a million dollars trembling in the balance, he would be deeply grateful if I would dispense with windy reports and simply FIND PARKER, DEAD OR ALIVE!

The rest of the letter said that Mrs. P. thought her husband spoke Spanish, of a kind, but she didn't know where he had learned it and didn't give a damn. Nobody had recognized the kid's picture. Parker's passport had been issued in Los Angeles but the file was in Washington and Adams was having trouble blasting a copy of the photograph loose from the State Department, who wanted to know what, why and wherefore. As soon as he got it, he would send it along. He didn't want me to wait for the picture before getting back to work.

The kid's photograph was beginning to look a little

frayed. I cut up one of those cellophane envelopes you carry your driver's license in and made a frame, binding the edges all around with scotch tape. Then I sat down and tried to figure what I ought to do.

My idea was still Chile. But it was only an idea, and Chile covered a lot of landscape. I could see myself stopping strange *chilenos* on the street and saying, "Excuse me, mister, but do you know a man named Robert R. Parker who might call himself Roberto Ruíz except that he probably isn't using either name? I don't know what name he is using or what he looks like or whether he is here in Chile at all or anything else about him, but I'd sure appreciate it if you could lead me to him." Until I had a decent picture I might pass him on the street every day for a month and never know whether I was on the right trail or just wasting my time while he sat under a coffee tree somewhere in Brazil. And a hunch has to be pretty strong if you are going to ride it as far as from Mexico to Chile.

Mine was strong. I packed all my clean shirts. Then I spent two days and another five hundred dollars of Adams' client's money getting a Chilean visa and a plane ticket to Santiago.

I had to switch from Pan-American to a Panagra plane at Balboa. I didn't have a Panamanian visa, but I was allowed twenty-four hours on my ticket for the stopover. I stretched it to cover the time from eight o'clock one night, when Pan-American dumped me off at Albrook Field, to three o'clock in the morning a day and a half later, when Panagra assumed the responsibility of transporting me and my clean shirts south-ward. I used up three of the clean shirts shuttling back and forth between Panama City and Cristóbal trying to get a line on Parker through the consulates.

It was hotter than hell, sand flies gnawed chunks out of me whenever I stood still for two seconds, and I didn't get anywhere. I couldn't cover all the consulates in one working day, but I tried the probables, including Chile. My hunch checked, in a negative way. Nobody had ever heard of Robert R. Parker.

The Panagra plane reached Santiago late the follow-ing afternoon, after flying along miles and miles of the most godawful desert coastline you ever saw in your life. There are deserts in Mexico, and I've crossed the Mojave in California, but they were alfalfa fields com-pared to Peru and northern Chile. Mile after mile of dirt hills with never a blade of grass or a tree, not a cactus plant or a dot of scrub for hours at a time except where a ribbon of dusty green lay along some stream trickling down out of the mountains, then more hours of bare dirt. It wasn't even sand, like an honest desert, but dirt, as dead as a landscape on the moon. Just watching it grind by from the plane window discouraged me. I didn't even perk up when the scenery finally changed and we flew in over the vineyards and orchards of Chile's central valley to come down at the Santiago air-port.

It was spring there—November. The fruit trees were in blossom. You could smell perfume in the breeze. The air was so clear that skyscrapers poking up from the middle of the city looked like something painted on a back drop. Going through the immigration gate, I asked one of the officials what Santiago's current population was.

"A million."

"And of Chile as a whole?"

"Five million, more or less."

"A populous country."

"Truly. You intend to stay here for some time, *señor*?"

"Several weeks, probably."

"Your business?'

"I gather needles. From haystacks."

I don't know what made me say it. I was feeling so low that I couldn't do anything but wisecrack. He didn't get the joke, so I told him I was a *turista* and let it go at that.

I got a room at the Hotel Carrera and went to work as soon as I had caught up on my sleep.

If you look at Chile on the map, you see a strip of bacon stretching twenty-five hundred miles up the west coast of South America between the Andes and the sea. Arica is at the upper end, Punta Arenas is at the bottom, and Santiago is in the middle. What you don't see on a map is the concentration of population in the Central Valley, which is a kind of transplanted Southern California set down between the desert of the north and the cold country of the south. One fifth of all Chilenos live in Santiago, and most of the others aren't far away. The whole country centers on the capital; industry, finance, transport, social life, everything. It's like Rome; all roads go there. Parker might not be in Santiago, but there was no better place to start looking for him.

To take care of the obvious, I called at the United States embassy and asked for information about Robert, or Roberto, Ruíz Parker, U.S. citizen. They didn't have him on the list. They suggested I try the consulate.

I tried the consulate. They didn't have anything on him, either. However, there were other consular offices at Arica, Antofagasta, Concepción, Punto Arenas, Valdivia, and Valparaíso. I could try them if I wanted to.

I said thanks very much and tried the local phone book instead.

There were several Parker's and a lot of Ruíz's in the phone book. Chile is so full of foreign blood, German and Irish and English and Swedes and what not who came into the country in the early days, that a name like Parker is not much more uncommon than it would be in the States. And Ruíz is the Spanish equivalent of Jones. But family ties are closer there. I figured that if my man had any right to either name, I ought to get something by spading.

I spaded for nearly two weeks. It wasn't fun. I telephoned people, called on them, wheedled them, bullied them, bribed their neighbors, lied about my business when a lie seemed better than the truth, and learned a lot of things including some juicy scandal. It left me with a bad taste in my mouth and no news of Robert Ruíz Parker. About all I accomplished was to spread the word around Santiago that I was looking for him, for reasons of my own, and would pay for information.

The second Saturday, after a rough week of getting nowhere, I decided to take the train down to Viña del Mar and spend the weekend lying on the sand.

Viña del Mar is a beach resort about ten minutes from Valparaíso, the main Chileno seaport. Valparaíso is three hours by train from Santiago. I was in Valparaíso before noon, and I knew that the consulate there would be open. I stopped in to ask my usual questions so my conscience wouldn't hurt too bad about taking the weekend off.

The consul was a young fellow, about my age, only balder. The minute I walked into his office he said, "Al, you old son of a bitch! What are you doing here?" so I figured we must have met before. With a little help, I remembered that his name was Lee and that we had played golf together in Mexico City when he was attached to the consulate there, three or four years before. Now he was consul in Valpo.

We talked about golf for a while. He belonged to a club near the city, and he invited me to play. He said I'd find it different from Mexico City, because he had lost fifty yards from his drives since coming down to sea-level. I said I didn't have any sticks along, and anyway I wanted to lie in the sun and do nothing for a couple of days. I had been working pretty hard.

"Working at what?"

"I'm looking for a guy."

"What's his name?"

"I don't know. He called himself Parker and Ruíz

and Ruíz Parker at various times. He probably isn't calling himself that now. I stopped in to see if you had any record of him."

"American?"

"He carried a United States passport."

"I'll see."

Lee rang a buzzer and asked somebody to go through the files. While we waited, he wanted to know where I was staying. I told him I had a hotel room in Santiago.

"When are you going back?"

"Sunday afternoon, probably."

"Good. I'll drive you up. The ambassador is giving his Thanksgiving party Sunday night. Everybody is invited."

"Thanksgiving?"

I hadn't realized that the winter holidays were coming on. Spring was busting out on every tree, there in Chile. In the streets, the high sun made you squint to shut out the glare.

"Sure. Every American in the country goes to the ambassador's Thanksgiving party. If your man is an American, he'll show up."

"He won't be advertising his citizenship."

"Come along anyway. It's the big party of the year and the ambassador expects everybody to stop in for a drink. I'll introduce you to some girls."

I said that would be fine. His man came back to report that there wasn't anything on Ruíz Parker in the files. I made a date to meet Lee the next afternoon, and then went on to Viña del Mar and rented myself a beach cottage.

The weekend did me a lot of good. I dozed a lot in the sun, got more sunburn than I needed, and didn't think too much about what a hopeless job I had. Lee picked me up late Sunday afternoon.

The party was going strong when we got to the embassy in Santiago. A lot of cars were lined up outside, and the place bulged with people standing thigh to thigh, like peanuts in a bowl. Everything was decorated with crepe-paper corn shucks and artificial pumpkins and cardboard turkey cut-outs, just like home. It seemed particularly strange because the evening was so warm and summery. Spring flowers were everywhere; in vases, in the corsages the women wore, and in floral displays made up in the shape of the American flag and the Chileno flag. The joint smelled like a cross between a conservatory and a barroom.

Somebody shoved a glass of champagne in my hand as soon as we got inside. The crush was so bad that I had to hold the glass over my head while I followed Lee through the mob to where the ambassador was telling a joke to a bunch of girls. The ambassador looked happy. I didn't blame him. Any time I have a dozen good-looking dolls standing around me in a circle laughing at my jokes, I'm happy, too.

Lee horned in to the circle to introduce me to the ambassador. The ambassador stopped telling stories long enough to say I was welcome and then introduced Lee and me to the girls. I didn't catch any of the names, but I said I was very pleased to meet everyone. When the ambassador had got his laugh on the next story, I backed out of the circle and moved over toward the wall where I could look around.

I didn't know what I was looking for. I just wanted to do something beside stand there with a glass in my hand. Lee, being official, had to circulate among the guests. That left me alone by the wall. After a while one of the girls who had been listening to the ambassador turned around, saw me there, smiled, and began to push her way toward me through the crowd.

Until then, I hadn't really noticed her. But when she came toward me, smiling, I knew I had seen her somewhere before that party. It was the same thing that had happened when I first bumped into Lee at the consulate; I didn't know the girl's name or where I had met her, but I knew her. The difference was that, with Lee, there hadn't been any particular reason for me to remember him. This girl was something else.

When she had worked her way through the crush to where I was standing, she said, "You seem lonelee, Mr. Colbee."

From her accented English, I guessed she was *chilena*. I looked at the ring finger of her left hand and said, in Spanish, "I am lonely no longer, *señorita*."

She smiled at that.

"You speak excellent *castellano* for a North American. You are North American, are you not?"

"Yes. But I was born in Mexico. I lived much of my life there."

"What do you do here in Chile?"

"I had heard of the beauty of your country and its women. I wished to see for myself. Now I believe what I was told."

It was the kind of talk that sounds corny in English but is a perfectly natural way to stall a conversation along in Spanish. And I was stalling, trying to place the girl.

She was a streaky blonde. There are plenty of blondes in Chile, and redheads, too, because many of the best families are descended from the O'Higgenses and O'Brien's and Kirchbachs and MacIvers and MacKennas who had a hand in settling the country. When I say she was streaky, I don't mean a bad peroxide job. She had the kind of light hair that bleaches even lighter in the sun, so that it looks like two shades of molasses taffy mixed together. Her eyes were light brown, and her skin was a golden tan. Her profile was something the Greeks would have tried to copy in marble. I couldn't understand how I could have forgotten her.

I said, "My memory fails me as I grow older, *señorita*. Have we not met before?"

"Of course." She pointed toward the ambassador, still holding court across the room. "We were introduced."

"Before that. Were you ever in Mexico?"

"No."

"The States?"

"No. But I have been to Paris and London."

"I have not. Yet I am sure I have seen you before."

She smiled—I forgot to mention that she had beautiful

teeth—and said, "At the *cine*?"

I didn't get it. She said, "I have been told I look like Mapy Cortés."

That was it. Mapy Cortés was a Mexican movie star, and a pretty flossy one to look at. I had seen Mapy's map so often on Mexican billboards that meeting it more or less in the flesh had puzzled me.

We talked some more. I still didn't know her name. When our glasses were empty, I went hunting for a waiter.

She was still there by the wall when I got back. So was a dark, husky young lad with a mustache and a gabardine suit I wouldn't have minded owning. They stopped talking when came up with the champagne.

The girl said, "Mister Colbee, I want you to meet my brother, Fito Ruano."

We couldn't shake hands, because both of mine were still full of champagne, but we said Hello and Some party, isn't it? Fito spoke English with the same accent as his sister; good, but neither American nor British. They had learned it in school.

Just by accident, I saw the look the girl gave him after we had stood there gassing for five minutes. He said, "The waiters have all broken their legs, and I want a drink. Excuse me, please?"

He grinned at me as he went away.

I waited for the pot to boil. Nothing happened.

I said, "Your name is also Ruano, then?"

"Of course."

"It is hard to catch names when so many come at

once. But I shouldn't have missed yours."

"Ruano is not a common name in Chile."

"You are *chilena*?"

"Yes. But my family came from Bolivia, originally."

Before I could take it from there, somebody grabbed my arm. It was Lee, stretching around two other people to reach me.

"There's an American over here named Parker. Want to meet him?"

"Sure. Excuse me, Miss Ruano?"

"Certainly."

I pushed my way through the crowd behind Lee to meet the American named Parker.

He was an engineer, just down from the States, six feet two of Yankee. He didn't have any relatives in Chile, didn't know any Ruíz's, and belonged to the Rotary club in Buffalo, New York. It took me five or ten minutes to get away from him. I didn't expect to find the streaky blonde where I had left her, but I went back to my corner anyway.

She was still there.

"I thought you had abandoned me." She flashed her wonderful teeth.

"That would have been not only ungentlemanly but foolish of me," I said. "Will you take another champagne?"

"No, thank you. Why were you so anxious to meet a man named Parker?"

"A matter of business."

"What is your business?"

I hadn't been hiding it for two weeks. I said, "I look for a man named Roberto Ruíz Parker. Have you ever heard the name?"

She wrinkled her forehead.

"No. Who is he?"

"A man I want to talk to."

"He is in Chile?"

"I think so."

"I do not know him. But we have Ruíz Guerra, Ruíz Spindola, Ruíz Montúfar, Ruíz Fulano, and Ruíz Tal y Tal. Possibly even Ruíz Parker."

We both laughed. Ruíz Fulano and Ruíz Tal y Tal were like saying Ruíz Doakes and Ruíz So-and-So. It wasn't much of a joke, but she was a pretty girl.

We talked some more, about nothing in particular. The party began to get noisy as the champagne took hold. They make good champagne in Chile, a little sweet but with plenty of authority. People began to roam around more. My girlfriend nodded and said hello every few seconds as somebody passed our corner. But she didn't leave me until her brother came by, hooked her by the arm, apologized to me for taking her away, and disappeared into the crowd. She waved goodbye over her shoulder.

I looked over the crowd, hunting for Lee. It was time to go.

Five minutes later my girlfriend was back. I was still trying to find Lee in the crowd, and I saw her coming. She had about five thousand dollars worth of mink wrapped around her. When she got near the edge of the mob, she put out her hand to me.

I took it. She said, "I do not like to think of your being lonely in my city, Mister Colbee. Will you come to tea tomorrow? About four?"

She disappeared before I could answer.

I looked at the card she had left in my hand. It was engraved: María Teresa Ruano Tarracena. On the back she had written an address on Avenida O'Higgins.

A waiter went by about then. I speared a drink off his tray and did a piece of heavy thinking.

You have to know Latin American social codes to understand why I wondered about María Teresa Ruano Tarracena. In Chile, the idea of a respectable girl sneaking a card into the hand of a strange man she had met at a party and asking him to call on her the next afternoon was crazy. Well-to-do *chilenas*, as a class, are pretty, intelligent, sophisticated, well-educated, speak three or four languages, and can pull their own weight in any gathering anywhere from Buenos Aires to Moscow. One thing they don't do is pick up strange men. Even assuming that María Teresa was so fascinated by my profile that she had to see it again soon, she should have asked her mother or her father, or whoever was head of her household, whether it was O.K. before she invited me to her home. I wondered if big brother Fito had given her the go-ahead, and why.

The crush kept getting thicker and noisier while I was studying the card, trying to fit María Teresa in with the other facts I kept stored away in a naturally suspicious mind. Somebody in the middle of the mob was giving a pretty good imitation of a turkey just before an execution *chileno* style, after the bird has been filled full of whiskey to relax his muscles and is staggering around under the ax drunker than a hoot-owl. The act was getting a lot of laughs, but it made the crowd bulge in my direction. One bulge, a nice-looking female rear, hit the glass in my hand before I could get it out of the way.

She jumped and said, "Oh, damn!" as the iced champagne soaked her skirt.

I said, "I'm sorry," handing her my handkerchief.

"It was my fault. I should have looked where I was going."

She got back against the wall and swabbed at her skirt.

I said, "I hope it doesn't stain."

"Don't sound so worried. It happens all the time in this country." She looked up at me, smiling. "New York?"

"California. I can do better than that with you. Kansas."

She shook her head.

"Pretty close. Idaho. What are you doing in Chile?"

"Working. What are you doing here?"

"Working."

We introduced ourselves.

Her name was Ann Farrell. She had a job in the foreign exchange department of the National City Bank branch there in Santiago, and she was friendly without being too friendly for a cocktail party pickup. She was a nice kid. I enjoyed talking to her. She had a lot of dark curly hair and an Irish map with a snub nose. When she smiled, it was different from my *chilena* girlfriend's smile; not so much voltage behind it, but more warmth.

We talked mostly about the people at the party. She pointed out some of the big shots to me—the Ministers of So and So and This and That were all there. Society was always well represented at the ambassador's Thanksgiving party.

"Maybe you're society yourself," Idaho said. "I saw you talking to Terry Ruano."

"I thought his name was Fito."

"Fito's sister. María Teresa."

"Oh. Do you know her?"

"In a business way. Her family keeps its money in my bank."

"Is she society?"

Idaho looked shocked.

"You *are* a stranger, aren't you! The Ruanos wouldn't talk to the Cabots and the Lodges if they came all the way from Boston to leave calling cards."

"Exclusive?"

"Like a safe-deposit vault. Where did you meet Terry?"

"I had a letter of introduction."

"It must have been from God."

I laughed and changed the subject.

Idaho had a boyfriend with her. He claimed her from me after the dying-turkey routine was finished. His name was Joe or Harry or Pete, and I never saw him again. But when I said goodbye to Idaho, and that I hoped to see her again before I left Chile, I really meant it. I liked her.

Lee pushed his way through the crowd a few minutes after Idaho had gone. He wiped the sweat off his face and said, "Let's get out of here."

We said good night to the ambassador and shoved our way out. I was tucking Terry Ruano's card away in my wallet, next to the kid's picture in its cellophane frame, when Lee said, "Make any progress?"

"I'm not sure. Maybe,"

"This isn't the States, boy. Handle her gently."

"Who?"

"Terry Ruano. The yum-yum you were talking to for half an hour. How did you manage to corner her like that?"

"She cornered me."

He wagged his head.

"Boy, you must have something that I don't know about. What's your secret?"

I said, "I wish I knew." I wasn't kidding, either.

5

THERE WERE STILL a lot of Ruíz's and Parkers for me to investigate in Santiago. I worked at it until four o'clock the next afternoon, not learning anything new, and then went calling.

The Ruano house was a family mansion, as I had suspected from the Avenida O'Higgins address. It included eighty-four thousand dollars worth of architecture and landscaping on the west side of town. From the outside, it reminded me of some of those big old museums overlooking the bay from Pacific Heights in San Francisco, where my grandfather, Hardshell Colby, took my grandmother, a Tlascan Indian girl named Sacúj, to crash society before she had learned to wear shoes. I knew how my grandmother had felt about it when I walked up a long curving driveway to the house, like a delivery boy, and whanged the knocker on the big front door.

A maid swung the door open after a while. I asked for the Señorita María Teresa. The maid said Pass yourself in. I passed myself in.

Somebody in the family had pesos, all right. Personally I have never liked big, quiet, gloomy places with thick carpets, marble statues crouching in the corners, oil paintings on the walls, and uncomfortable chairs costing seven hundred and fifty dollars each, but it was pretty elegant. The maid left me in a big *sala* sucking my thumb for a while with the statues, and then came back to lead me off through another wing of the museum to where an archway and three steps led down to a pretty little *patio*, full of lawn and flower beds, with a couple of love birds in a cage hanging from a tree.

María Teresa was there. So were some teacups, a plateful of those little turnovers called *empanadas,* and big brother Fito. Fito stood up to shake hands when I came out in the *patio.*

María Teresa said, "It was good of you to come."

"It was good of you to ask me."

"Sit down, please. We were having tea. Would you like something stronger?"

I said tea would be fine. She poured a cup for me and gave me an *empanada.*

She was wearing one of those plain black dresses that have no decorations on them, no fancy stitching, and all the style in the world. With the dress she wore an old-fashioned gold bracelet and a pair of matching earrings. I could see that her ears had been pierced for the earrings, because she had her hair fixed up on top of her head. The sun shining on it made it look like a twist of the *melaza* candy they sell in Chapultepec Park, gleaming yellow streaks in lighter gleaming brown, gold and bronze run together. With the plain black dress to set off her hair and her eyes—they were honey-colored, not brown, as I had thought—she was a knockout.

We talked about the weather, switching back and forth between English and Spanish. They both spoke English freely, although with the schoolbook accent I had noticed before. Fito said I spoke good Spanish for a North American. I told him about being born in Mexico and spending most of my life there.

He said, "But you are *estadounidense*?"

"Yes. My father saw to that."

"He was *estadounidense*?"

"Yes."

"I should like to go to the United States some day," María Teresa said wistfully. "My father does not want me to go. He thinks the States are uncivilized."

She was a honey, all right. She made me want to run out and buy her a ticket, and the hell with her father. I swallowed another mouthful of tea.

The love birds grumbled in their cage. Fito said, "You travel a lot?"

"Some. On business."

"What is your business?"

"At present I am searching for a man named Robert Ruíz Parker."

I was watching Fito's knuckles. They tightened.

"Why do you search for him?"

"A business matter."

"What kind of business?"

Instead of answering him, I reached for another *empanada* and told María Teresa how good they were. She thanked me without looking at me. I said I certainly enjoyed *chileno* cooking; *empanadas, cazuela de ave, porotos granados, turrón,* the rest of it. Yes, indeedy.

All this was to make Fito come to me wide open. I was twitching all over waiting for him to ask his question again. For a minute I thought I had scared him off, because both he and María Teresa looked uncomfortably at their shoes while the love birds cursed each other. I cursed myself. Then Fito tried again.

"What kind of business do you have with Roberto Ruíz Parker?"

"I would have to know your own interest before I could tell you that."

They looked sideways at each other. María Teresa nodded.

Fito said awkwardly, "My uncle used that name once. His real name was Roberto Ruano Parker. He is dead."

I damn near jumped out of my chair and kicked my heels. Instead, I said, "I'm sorry. When did he die?"

"Several years ago."

"How did he die?"

"It was . . . "

"I think it would be better if my father told you about it," María Teresa put in. *"¿Con permiso?"*

I said the permission was hers. She rang a bell. When the maid showed up, María Teresa told her to request the presence of don Rodolfo in the *patio.*

While we waited, María Teresa was careful not to look in my direction. We were both thinking the same thing. She had lied to me about not knowing the name

Robert Ruíz Parker, and it made her miserable because I knew she had lied. I was just worried. My hunch had paid off, and I had my lead on Parker, but I didn't like the way it was being handed to me. It was too much like having the guy at the carnival lift the left-hand shell to show me that the pea was really there in case I wanted to make a heavy bet on the next shuffle.

Don Rodolfo, when he showed up, was right out of a picture by Velasquéz. He wore an old jacket with oil paint on it, but he would have looked at home in a *charro* costume covered with gold embroidery. His gray hair was going white, and he had a white clipped beard and mustache. He was the Spanish grandee from Grandeeville.

I stood up to shake hands. He apologized, in Spanish, for his appearance. María Teresa said, "My father speaks very little English. If you will be so kind . . . "

"Certainly."

The Spanish grandee looked politely from me to Fito to María Teresa, waiting for somebody to toss him the ball.

María Teresa said, "Señor Colby has come to Chile in search of Roberto Ruíz Parker."

The Spanish grandee lifted an eyebrow.

"What is your interest in my brother?"

I told him what I felt like telling him; that I was a private investigator and that I had been retained by a lawyer in the United States to find Robert Ruíz Parker or determine that he was dead. Since they had told me he was dead, I would appreciate it if they would give me further information about the date and circumstances of his death, the disposition of his body, and so forth. I would have to check the facts.

Without any heat in his voice, the Spanish grandee said, "Do you question our word, *señor*?"

"No *señor*. For myself, I am satisfied. But the matter involves certain properties to which your brother held title. The courts of my country accept no man's unsupported word."

"What are these properties?" Fito asked.

I didn't know whether to answer that one or not. Until I got more information, all I had to trade with was what I knew. Before I could think up an answer that wouldn't hurt anybody's feelings, don Rodolfo said mildly, "You need not concern yourself too much with the affairs of your uncle, Fito."

He was the boss, all right. Fito took it like a good boy. The Spanish grandee said to me, "Perhaps you would honor us with your presence here tomorrow night for dinner. Afterwards we can play billiards and discuss this matter. Do you play billiards?"

I said I knew the principle of the game. The Spanish grandee said he would be honored with my company at eight the next night. I said I would be honored to attend. We shook hands all around. That was that.

María Teresa went with me to the door. She was still feeling bad because I had caught her in a lie, so I told her how much I had enjoyed her hospitality and chattered away like a chipmunk until she decided I had forgotten it. In the end, I got myself a wonderful smile, said *hasta mañana,* and went down the driveway feeling as gloomy as any man would feel when a beautiful girl with molasses-taffy hair and honey-colored eyes smiles at him as if she meant it and he knows all the time that he is being suckered.

6

BECAUSE it was obvious that I was being suckered. And even if I agreed with myself that I had a nasty low suspicious mind and probably an inferiority complex four miles wide because I suspected dirty work every time a pretty girl smiled at me, I was *still* being suckered.

Look at it this way. I had spent two hard weeks prowling around Santiago asking nosy questions about Robert Ruíz Parker. I hadn't learned anything about him, but a lot of people had heard about old Bulldog Colby, the hawkshaw with the grim jaw, and been told what a determined little rascal he was. Old Bulldog Colby was liable to learn something if he kept at it. There were two things that could be done with old Bulldog Colby. If it didn't matter what he found out, why then let him sweat until he found it out or else get in touch with him and tell him what there was to tell. That didn't mean he had to be invited out to dinner at a home that was too exclusive for the Cabots and the Lodges, either, but if feeding him a meal seemed like the proper thing, all anybody had to do was look him up at the Hotel Carrera and say "My name is so and so. I hear that you are interested in Robert Ruíz Parker. Come out to dinner and I'll tell you about him." That was the easy way.

But what had happened? A sweet young thing sort of accidentally meets me at a party which every *estadounidense* in Santiago could be expected to attend. We talk. I like to talk to her. So would any one of four hundred other men at the party, all better-looking than I am, but she devotes herself to me until she learns that I am looking for a man by the name of Robert Ruíz Parker. She is not surprised to hear the name. She has never heard it before. But after she has had a chance to talk it over with her big brother, who is also at the party, she does not want me to be lonely in Santiago and invites me to her home. There it turns out that Robert Ruíz Parker is really her poor old dead uncle Roberto, about whom her father is going to explain tomorrow night, including the reason why she had denied ever having heard the name.

There would be plenty of explanations, I was willing to bet. For my money, they would all be horsefeathers.

That night I went to the movies. There was a crook picture at the Comedia. It was in English with Spanish subtitles, and it was pretty good, too, except that at the end the detective explained to the girl how he had known, ever since the clock stopped in the second reel, that the gardener had poisoned the soup, and I couldn't see it even after he explained it. I had a fat chance of figuring out what María Teresa's father was cooking up for me.

I gave up the Ruíz-Parker angle and spent the morning checking up on the Ruanos. A lot of people had heard the name, but nobody knew much about them except that the old folks were super-exclusive and didn't mingle much. The old man sculpted or painted or something. That was all I had time to learn.

In the afternoon I sent a cable off to Adams, asking him to hurry Parker's picture along when he got it. Then I had a *siesta*. When I walked up the long driveway to the museum at eight o'clock, I was in fair shape to catch whatever fast balls were coming my way.

I should have known better than to get here on time. Nobody does in Chile, and nobody is expected to. The family wasn't even dressed. The maid showed me into a *sala*—not the big one with the statues, but a smaller room with a wood fire in a grate—and left me there. After I had studied the shine on my shoes for half an hour, María Teresa came in.

I'm not good at noticing women's clothes, ordinarily, but I always noticed hers. The way she wore them, I had to. That night she had on a turquoise-green job, an evening dress with a long skirt jimmied around some way to look like a pair of those harem pants the girls wear in movies about Arabia, only more ladylike. Her arms, her neck, and what I could see of her back and the rest of her was the same golden tan as her face, smooth and brown like old silk. The family museum probably had a sun-deck where she spent long hours getting those streaks in her hair and earning the tan, because I didn't see any of the marks a bathing suit would have left on her. I found myself dreaming up a picture of her lying on the sun-deck. It wasn't a nice way to look at my hostess, but I couldn't help it.

She had a cocktail brought in for me, and a *naran-jada* for herself. We talked about the weather and prospects for a good ski-season in the mountains next winter. She liked to ski. She also played tennis and golf and rode horses. I said I played golf. Maybe we could have a game some time. She thought that would be fine. I thought it would be fine, too. Lovely weather we're having, isn't it?

Fito, the old man and María Teresa's ma came in together. Fito and don Rodolfo were in evening clothes. Don Rodolfo looked like a Grand Duke. We both started to apologize, I because I didn't have any evening clothes and he because he had been stupid not to realize that I wouldn't have brought them along on a business trip. He and Fito would change right away. I talked them out of it, after an Alphonse-and-Gaston argument.

The old lady was another character. Her name was doña María. I supposed that María Teresa had been named after her. She was old-school Latin, dark going gray, with a faint mustache and maybe a little dumpier through the hips than was stylish but a very nice old dame. She welcomed me to her home with four or five words of pretty bad English. I came back in Spanish, she commented on my *castellano,* and I had to explain all over again about being born in Mexico, a very nice country but nothing to compare with Chile. We went on from there, tossing chitchat and compliments around the circle at each other, drinking cocktails poured from a silver shaker, as cozy as a family of worms in a knot.

All this about clothes and cocktails and chitchat is to

show what a smooth shell game they had rigged up for me. It was perfect. I couldn't have felt more at home in my mother's lap. They laughed at my jokes, poured cocktails into me, kept the conversation pointed my way, and managed to make me feel that the Ruano household had just been holding its breath waiting for me to come along. When dinner was served, they sat me on don Rodolfo's right, the place of honor. Fito was next to me, María Teresa across the table, doña María at the end. I think a more customary eating arrangement would have been to put me next to María Teresa, but as it was I had to look at her, watch the light of the candles on the dinner table gleam on her golden skin and bring out the flecks in her honey-colored eyes and glints on her teeth when she laughed. She laughed a lot. Everybody did. There was plenty of good food, with good *chileno* wine to wash it down, and when the Ruanos weren't showing me what a swell guy they thought I was, they were doing the same thing for each other. That part, at least, was the real McCoy. The family was a mutual-admiration society. You could tell just by watching them that they thought their old man was the nicest old man, their old lady the nicest old lady, and the two kids the nicest brother and sister ever born. After a few *copitas* of wine, I began to agree with them. It was good to meet a family like that. Until then, the job had been too full of people like Molly Jean Mendoza and Parker's slut of a wife in Pasadena.

Thinking about Parker snapped me out of my rosy glow. I would have to watch myself.

Parker's name had not been mentioned once. I knew it wasn't good manners to discuss business matters when the ladies were present, so I waited. After coffee, don Rodolfo and I excused ourselves and went downstairs to the billiard room. Fito wasn't invited to play.

There were a number of paintings on the wall of the billiard room. They were all small, mostly still-lifes with a lot of fine detail, but one was a pretty good picture of the *patio* where I had had tea the day before. A lot of work had gone into that painting. You could even see the tiny love birds in their cage.

I said to don Rodolfo, "These are your own?"

"My own poor efforts, yes."

"They seem very good to me. That of the *patio* is excellent."

"It is yours."

He went over to the wall to take it down.

It had been a long time since I had met anyone who still observed the old tradition which requires a Spanish *caballero* to offer to his guest anything which the guest admires in the *caballero's* home. But I still remembered the answers, so I got out of it. The picture stayed on the wall where it belonged. I was careful not to admire the billiard table.

We shucked off our coats and rolled up our sleeves.

"Do you play three cushions?" don Rodolfo said, offering me first crack at the cue rack with a gesture Don Quixote would have used handing somebody a sword.

"Not well."

"Then we will play straight rail."

He chalked up his cue as I made the break.

I would not like to have played the old boy for money. He ran eight billiards together on his first string. After he got warmed up he was putting strings of twelve and fifteen together as easily as I made two. He was too good a player to miss a shot deliberately but I saw him try several four- or five-cushion shots that could have been made an easier way, and I knew he was going easy on me. While he was chalking his cue for a particularly tough one he said, "How much do you know of the man who called himself Robert Ruíz Parker."

"He was married for about fifteen years, under the name of Robert R. Parker, to a woman in Pasadena, California. He deserted her five years ago, obtained an American passport by swearing to United States citizenship, journeyed around Central and South America for a time to conceal his trail, and came to Chile. He left with his wife the properties I spoke of yesterday, but the law of the country in which they lived makes it impossible for her to dispose of them without his consent as long as he is alive. I was instructed to persuade him to communicate with his wife's lawyer or to bring back sufficient evidence to prove to the courts that he is dead."

Don Rodolfo made three billiards while I was talking. He missed the fourth one. I chalked my cue and took over.

"What can you tell me about Robert R. Parker?" I said.

"He was my brother. His name was Roberto Ruano. Parker was our mother's name. He left Chile as a young man and went to the States, where, as you say, he married. I did not hear from him while he was gone. I knew nothing of him, not that he was alive or dead, until he came back. He did not talk much of himself, except to say that his life had been unhappy and he wished to avoid discovery by his wife. He would not discuss it further. I helped him buy a *fundo,* a farm, near Melipilla, a small town fifteen or twenty leagues southwest of here. He died there shortly after his return. His body lies on his farm, the Hacienda Quilpué."

"How did he die?"

"We do not know, for sure. He was in the habit of riding alone over his farm. One time he did not return. When he was found, his horse lay dead beside him, a bullet through its skull. The bullet had come from my brother's pistol, which was empty. We think that the horse fell—it was a remote, dangerous part of the *fundo*—and injured both itself and him. He would have put it out of its misery and then used the other shots in the pistol to try to attract help. It did not come in time to save him."

"He did not keep a bullet for himself, perhaps?"

"That we do not know. It was nearly two weeks before he was found. The buzzards had done things to him which made the exact manner of his death impossible to discover."

The old man's voice was as level as ever. But I straightened up from missing my billiard in time to see his face.

I said, "I am sorry to distress you, don Rodolfo. It is

my duty to learn all there is to know."

"Do not distress yourself on my account. I am at your service."

"It is your play."

He ran a string of ten smooth billiards together like falling off a log.

It was a nice, neat, believable story, so far. Not a bug in a carload. I said, "Did you ever consider that your brother might have been murdered?"

"It was considered by the authorities. I do not believe it, myself. He had no enemies. Nor friends."

"You can not know what enemies he made while he was away, don Rodolfo. And men have been killed for the money they carried in their pockets."

"It is a possibility."

"He was a wealthy man?"

"Yes. Our money came from the nitrate fields. In the old days, before the Germans learned to—*hacerlo*—there is an English word . . . "

"Synthesize."

"Yes. Before the Germans learned to synthesize, there was great wealth in the nitrate fields. Even afterwards, profits could be made. He himself had done all the work of developing the family holdings, which were in his name—he was the elder son, you understand, and the properties came to him from my father—but we shared the income. When he returned, money was waiting which I had held for him in trust. It was more than enough to buy the *fundo* and provide for his old age—even had his old age not been so brief."

He missed the eleventh billiard by a hair off the fourth cushion, and clicked his tongue.

"My eye is failing. Fito does not give me enough practice."

"For that I am grateful. The properties descended to you then?"

"By Chilean law. He had no other heirs."

"There is the wife in California."

He watched me make a billiard. Two billiards. Three billiards. Four. It was one of my longest strings.

He said slowly, "My brother told me that he left her well provided for. I do not think she has any just claim against properties which have been in my family for generations."

"She will certainly be well provided for if the matter of title to the California properties is clarified. That is the reason—the only reason—I am here in Chile."

He didn't say anything to that.

While I was gnawing over what he had told me, he ran out his string. Then we had brandy which a *muchacho* brought down to us from upstairs. I didn't know if any more billiards were coming up, and I was ready to bite off another chew.

"You will help me obtain the evidence I need to prove your brother's death, don Rodolfo?"

"Certainly. I am at your service."

"Who found the body?"

"A *vaquero* on his farm."

"Who identified it?"

"The *vaquero* first. I saw it later."

"You are certain of the identification? I say because you mentioned the buzzards. . ."

"I am certain. There was—enough—remaining—for me to be sure."

His face was stony.

"It lies on the *fundo* now?"

"Yes. There is a small graveyard."

"Under what name was he buried?"

"His own. Roberto Ruano Parker."

"How will I be able to prove that Roberto Ruano parker of Chile and Robert R. Parker of California were the same?"

He thought about it.

"I will give you a paper under oath that they were the same person."

"That will help. Who else knew of his identity?"

"My son and my daughter."

"Not doña María?"

"No. She knows only that he was in the States for a long time. She knows nothing of his—other life. I do not wish her to know more than she does."

"There is no need for her to know. Will your son and your daughter also give me a paper under oath?"

There was the faintest hesitation before he answered. "If you wish it."

"In the event your affidavits are not sufficient for the purposes of my client, will you give me authority to have the body disinterred?"

He frowned at me.

"What purpose would that serve? He has been dead

more than four years. By this time . . . "

"I have a report of a medical examination which includes a chart of his teeth. It would be certain identification."

He didn't answer.

I said, "I realize how distasteful the thought must be to you, don Rodolfo. I suggest it only because the affidavits may not satisfy California legal requirements. If they do, nothing further will be necessary. If they do not, I will need your cooperation."

He said slowly, "I hope that the affidavits will serve. My brother did not talk much of his life in the States, but I know that he wished to escape it completely. From what you tell me, he had much of which to be ashamed. His shame will be my family's shame if his grave is publicly opened and it becomes known that he was a wife-deserter and a liar under oath. He was not entitled to claim United States citizenship. He was *puro chileno,* as I am." Don Rodolfo lifted his old grandee's head. "I should not like to shame my family. We are proud— too proud, perhaps."

"I will do everything possible to save your pride. Can I count on your help, if it becomes necessary?"

"We will see."

He trounced me two more games of billiards, each time apologizing for his own good luck and complimenting me on my excellent game, as a *caballero* should. His home was mine to use whenever I liked. He was going to give me cards to the Club de la Unión, the Club de Septiembre, and a couple of others. He was going to break his back seeing that I had a real bang-up time while I was in Chile, and tomorrow he and the kids would meet me at the United States consul's office to make out the affidavits. We didn't talk any more about opening his brother's grave.

After the billiards, we joined María Teresa and her mother upstairs. Fito had gone out. We sniffed another brandy, talked for a while, and I left.

María Teresa went to the door with me again. We stopped off in the big front *sala* to wait while the maid brought my hat.

I said, "I'd like to ask you and your father and mother to go to dinner with me tomorrow, if you have no other plans."

"My father and mother never go out. But I'll tell them you asked."

"How about you?"

She didn't hesitate a minute.

"I'd like it. Will you wait until I ask my father?"

I said I'd wait. She went to check with the old man.

While I waited, I looked at the statues. Also the pictures. Some of them seemed to be pretty good stuff, and some were just things that belonged to the family, portraits of grandpa and Aunt Minnie and the others. There weren't any of the old man's private production.

One picture, a small photograph in a gilt frame, stood on a table near the door. I was holding it in my hand when María Teresa came back.

"Yes," she said. "What time will you call for me?"

"Seven-thirty?"

My voice must have shown something. She looked surprised when she said seven-thirty was fine. I held out the photograph.

"'Who is this?"

She laughed.

"I've grown a lot, haven't I? I was four years old when that was taken."

"You were a pretty child."

"Thank you."

I put the picture down. We said good night.

Back at the hotel I got the Parker stuff out of my bag and looked at the kid's picture I had framed with cellophane.

It was Fito, all right. I would have known they were brother and sister even if the two photographs hadn't had the same style, the same pose, the same solemn, scrubbed little-kid look. I hadn't recognized María Teresa only because she looked like Mapy Cortés. I had stared so hard and so often at her brother's picture as a small boy that the features had fixed themselves in my mind, so that although I hadn't been able to recognize him behind the mustache and twenty years of growing up, I could see the resemblance in her.

But why had Uncle Roberto, who had not thought enough of his brother to write a letter in twenty years, carried his nephew's picture with him so long and so faithfully before losing it in the front seat of the Buick?

I was sure getting plenty to chew on as I went along.

7

NEXT MORNING I sent another cable off to Adams. At first I tried to code it, in case the Ruanos had pipelines of their own which led to the cable office, but it got too complicated. I thought, what the hell, if they were checking me that close, the sooner we got out in the open the better.

I sent the cable straight. It was expensive. It read:

AM ON TRAIL. PARKER, ALIAS, REPORTED DEAD HERE SEVERAL YEARS AGO. CAN OBTAIN AFFIDAVITS TO SUBSTANTIATE IDENTITY, BUT EXPECT OPPOSITION TO DEMAND FOR EXHUMATION OF BODY FOR EXAMINATION. DON'T KNOW WHAT IS COOKING BUT SUSPECT SOMETHING SCREWY. WILL YOU ACCEPT AFFIDAVITS SUBSTANTIATING FACT OF DEATH OR SHALL I INQUIRE FURTHER INTO FACTS. EMPHASIZE THAT AM QUESTIONING AFFIDAVITS ON HUNCH ONLY. REQUEST INSTRUCTIONS AND ADDITIONAL 2500 EXPENSE MONEY CARE HOTEL CARRERA HERE IF FURTHER INVESTIGATION DESIRED. IN LATTER CASE, SUGGEST YOU REPLY WITH SIMPLE STATEMENT THAT AFFIDAVITS ARE INSUFFICIENT FOR YOUR PURPOSE AND AUTHORIZE FURTHER EXPENDITURE.

The last part was so that I would get something with which to squeeze don Rodolfo if I had to. The extra twenty-five hundred bucks wasn't essential at the moment, but I might need it sooner or later and I was half hoping that it might scare Adams into calling me off with the affidavits. I explained to the clerk at the cable office that "screwy" was an abbreviation for *una cosa loca,* then went to the consulate to keep my date with the Ruano family.

They were late. When they showed up, the consul was busy. We had to wait another half an hour before I could introduce don Rodolfo. The consul knew Fito and María Teresa already, but I could see that Idaho Farrell hadn't been kidding me when she said that the family was exclusive. Apparently this was the first time the old man had appeared in public since the big earthquake.

The consul spoke good Spanish, so nobody had to interpret. Don Rodolfo told him what they wanted to do. It was a family matter, he explained, *muy delicada,* and he trusted that the consul would understand that it was strictly private, not to go any further. The consul understood perfectly. He would even type the statements himself if they would write them out for him.

The old man wrote out a statement that I dictated. Then I dictated another for the two kids, and the consul sat down and beat them out on a typewriter while we waited.

The air was a little strained. We didn't talk much. When the consul had finished typing, he passed the papers around for signature, took their oaths, and slapped his seal on the documents. I put them in my pocket.

Things were easier after we got out in the street. I thanked them all for their help and so forth and reminded María Teresa of our date that night. She said she was looking forward to it. Fito wanted to know if there was anything he could do for me. Was I comfortable at my hotel? Would I like him to arrange a golf match for me? Would I like him to take me to the cockfights?

I said I was happy, thanks just the same. The Ruanos went their way and I went mine.

I spent the day wandering around town reading inscriptions on statues of O'Higgins and Simón Bolivar and José de San Martín and General O'Brien and all the others who had fought, bled and died to make Chile what it was. Santiago is a beautiful place at any time. On that particular spring afternoon, with the sun warm on my head, the birds singing in the trees and the odor of flowering fruit trees so strong that even the smell of horse traffic on the Alameda couldn't kill it, with the papers that ought to mark the completion of my job signed, sealed and delivered in my pocket, and having a date that night with a pretty girl, I should have been the most contented cow that ever wandered across the green grass of Parque Providencia down to the river bank to chew my cud and stare at the water. I wasn't. I felt like biting somebody's ear off.

That night, I drove up to the Ruano family mausoleum in a sporty green coupé I had rented. María Teresa was ready, a surprising thing for a South American girl. She brought along her five thousand dollars worth of mink, and a *mantilla* to tie over her hair. We drove up the Alameda, the breeze blowing fresh and fragrant through the windows of the coupé.

I said, "Where do you want to go?"

"Where do *you* want to go?"

"I don't know anything but the Carrera and the neighborhood around Plaza de Armas. I thought you might be able to suggest some place not too noisy where we could dance and have dinner and talk. Anything you like is all right with me."

She thought about it.

"Have you seen Cerro San Cristóbal?"

"No."

"Let's go there. There's a casino, and a view of the city. Turn off down this street."

We drove across the river and followed a winding road that took us a thousand feet up the *cerro* to a parking lot below the casino. After that we walked higher, up through a garden to where a big iron statue of the Virgin looked out over the city, a billion twinkling lights glowing beyond the river that ran across the foot of the hill. The night was as clear as crystal, and the garden around us still exhaled perfume after hours in the sun.

María Teresa breathed deeply.

"Have you ever seen anything so beautiful?"

"Mexico isn't bad. New York has its points, too. But I don't think Mexicans or New Yorkers feel as sentimental as you do about it."

"You think I am sentimental?"

She looked up at me. A light beyond my shoulder brought out the flecks in her eyes. Her lips, slightly parted, were as red as the fires of hell.

I said, "Everybody is sentimental at some time or another. Let's go down to the casino."

We could still see the lights of the city from the terrace where we had dinner. A couple of times we went inside the casino, where an orchestra was playing, to dance. I didn't ask her to dance very often. She was as light as a feather, and when I put my arms around her and smelled whatever she was wearing on her hair, I was afraid I might lose my grip. Whatever Adams' wire said the next day, I meant to square away with María Teresa that night.

After our last dance, we went back to the terrace for coffee. I took Fito's picture out of my pocket, holding it face down in my hand.

"Miss Ruano . . ."

"Please don't call me 'Miss.' All my good friends call me Terry. Or you can call me Maruja, as my mother does, or . . ."

"Terry is fine. I like Terry."

"How are you called?"

"Al."

"Ahl?" She couldn't get the flat A. "Is that a name?"

"It stands for Alvin, but I don't like it. Ahl will do."

"Ahlbin." She tried it, and nodded. "I like Ahlbin."

"Couldn't you make it Alfín?"

We both laughed at that. *Al fin* means "finally" or

"at last."

At last, I thought. What are you stalling for, you big chump? I took a deep breath.

"Terry, did you know your Uncle Roberto well— before he went away?"

She stopped laughing.

"Why do you ask?"

"I'm still working at my job."

I looked at the picture in my hand, and then at the lights of the city below the terrace. It was a beautiful spot to be sitting with a pretty girl.

She said, "I did not know him at all. I was only a baby when he went away. I can't even remember him, from those days."

"Do you have any recollection that he was particularly fond of your brother? That he brought him toys, or played with him, or paid him any particular attention that he did not pay you? Or has your family ever said that he was particularly fond of Fito as a baby?"

She shook her head, watching me.

"Then," I said, turning the picture over in front of her eyes, "Why do you suppose your uncle carried this photograph of Fito with him for fifteen years?"

I had put her where the lights from the casino would shine in her face. Seeing the picture cold turkey like that frightened her, before she could cover up. It was just plain fright, nothing else.

I could see her trying to think up an answer. Before she had time to work it out, I hit her again.

"And why, after you told me that you had never heard of Roberto Ruíz Parker, did you change your mind and invite me to your home so your father could tell me about your uncle, whose return to this country you all kept so well hidden until my arrival?"

She shook her head. I had rocked her enough, but I fired the third battery because it was eating at me and I couldn't help it.

"And finally, why are you being so nice to me? Did you like my appearance at the embassy? Or am I being kept happy on orders from don Rodolfo?"

Later I kicked myself plenty for the last one. It had nothing to do with the job. It was a dumb thing to say, from any viewpoint. I might even have got some kind of an answer to the other questions if I had kept my trap shut. Instead, she stood up.

"Will you take me home, please?"

I took her home.

We didn't talk going back to the car, we didn't talk during the drive, and she didn't want to wait for me to take her to her door. But I put my hand on her wrist before she could get out of the car.

"For the last question I asked, I apologize," I said. "It was a stupid thing to say. I am going to know the answers to the other questions before I leave Chile."

"Good night."

"Good night."

I let her go.

The *mozo* who gave me back my deposit on the coupé later that night went over the car pretty carefully first, the way they all do to see if there are any burns in the upholstery. There was a hairpin on the seat. He picked it up, grinning at me.

"A *rubia*," he said. "You had good luck with the car, friend?"

"Excellent luck," I said. "The best."

I bought a bottle of *pisco* on the way back to the hotel and killed it in my room, lying flat on my back on the bed looking at the dark.

8

FITO CALLED on me the next morning.

I was still in bed when he came. My match with the *pisco* bottle had left me feeling pretty rocky. Even at that low altitude, where a hangover doesn't hurt half as much as it does up in the mountains, I had a bad case of whips and jingles. When I creaked out of bed to open the door and saw Fito standing there, his jaw tight and his eyes hard, I thought he was going to take a poke at me.

I stepped back, ready to mill with him if his hands came up but not feeling enthusiastic about it. He walked into the room without taking off his hat.

"My father asked me to bring you these."

He held out a couple of cards.

They were the guest-cards the old man had promised me. I took them and saw that don Rodolfo Ruano was guaranteeing my credit at his clubs.

"Thanks. Sit down."

"No, thank you."

"Excuse me, then."

I poured myself a glass of water and sat down on the bed. Fito stood where he was, in the middle of the room, looking mad.

"My sister told me of your conversation last night. I thought I had better come talk to you."

I drank some of the water.

"I gather that you are not wholly satisfied with what we have done to help you."

His accent was thicker than usual, and he stumbled over a couple of words. I said, "Speak Spanish."

"I prefer English. I want to be sure that we understand each other. Why did you ask my sister those questions last night?"

I overlooked the crack at my Spanish, which was a lot better than his own, and answered his question.

"I wanted information."

"Have we not given you all the information you need? Are you not satisfied that we have helped you do what you came here to do? Do you expect to gain something by molesting my sister with insulting questions . . . ?"

"They weren't meant to be insulting."

"They were."

"They were not." I poured myself another glass of water. "If you want to make something personal out of it, go right ahead. But don't waste your time inventing insults that didn't take place. I wanted information. I asked for it. Your sister didn't answer me, that's all."

"Certainly not. Any questions that concern my family should be addressed to me, or to my father. My sister . . ."

"I'll address one to you now, then. Will you try to persuade your father to give me an authority to open your uncle's grave?"

"No!"

He didn't even stop to think. It came out as if I had punched him in the belly.

"Why not?"

"Because when a man dies, his body is put to rest. It is not laid away so that strangers can come along afterward and paw over his bones. Is that hard for you to understand?"

"I don't want to paw over his bones. I want a dentist to look at his teeth and tell me a few things."

"Why?"

"Because, as I explained to your father, the United States courts may not be willing to take anybody's word about the fact of death, under oath or otherwise, when the death involves title to a quarter of a million dollars worth of property, and more. If they don't take the affidavits, I've got to get facts. The best way I can get them is to open the grave."

"What is it to us what you want?" Fito shouted. His neck was getting red. "Is it a concern of ours what your courts need or do not need? My uncle was a *chileno*. He came home to die. Leave him in peace!"

"He claimed United States citizenship when he was in the United States," I said. "Also he deserted his wife. Disturbing the peaceful rest of the bones of a liar and a wife deserter doesn't worry me a hell of a lot."

I was needling him to see if he would get mad enough to spill something, but I thought for a minute he was going to bust me instead. I was still sitting on the bed. When he took a step toward me, I put both feet down flat and leaned forward, planning to come up inside anything he threw at me. He stood there for a minute, his neck swelling, his fists bunched. Then he turned on his heel and roared out of the room, leaving the door open.

A bellboy knocked on the door while I was shaving. He sold me two cablegrams for ten pesos each. I didn't know whether to feel good or bad after I had read them. The first one said:

MIGG (that meant "My good God!") DO I HAVE TO DO THE JOB MYSELF QUESTION MARK IF YOU CAN'T SATISFY YOURSELF YOU CAN'T SATISFY ME AND I CAN'T SATISFY A CALIFORNIA COURT STOP TIME IS OF THE ESSENCE STOP GET ME RESULTS AND PLEASE REPEAT PLEASE MAKE THEM RESULTS NOT GUESSES COMMA HUNCHES COMMA OR HEARSAY STOP IN OTHER WORDS COMMA IS HE OR ISN'T HE QUESTION MARK AM CREDITING TWENTY-FIVE HUNDRED YOUR ACCOUNT NATCITBANK THERE STOP THAT IS ALL IN EVERY SENSE OF THE WORD STOP HAVE NOT YET BEEN ABLE TO OBTAIN PICTURE BUT WILL FORWARD IT AS SOON AS POSSIBLE STOP

The other cable was what I had asked for. It said:

REGRET AFFIDAVITS INSUFFICIENT STOP REQUIRE FURTHER SUBSTANTIATION OF IDENTITY.

I got over to the bank in a hurry. I didn't need the money right away, but I wanted to get it out of hock before they glued it down. The official exchange rate, the bank rate, was about twenty-three for one, and I could get twice that on any street corner.

I had forgotten all about Idaho Farrell until I saw her at a desk in the foreign-exchange department of the bank. She saw me at about the same time. She got up from her desk and came over to where I was standing.

"Good morning, Mister Colby."

"Good morning, Miss Farrell."

"What can I do for you?"

"I have some dollars in your bank which I would like to get out of your clutches as soon as possible."

"How many dollars?"

"Twenty-five hundred."

"I'm afraid you'll have to take it out in pieces. We can't exchange more than five hundred at a time."

"I don't want exchange. I want dollars."

She laughed. "So does everyone else."

I said, "Look, can't we make a deal? I can get . . ."

". . . forty-seven for one on the free market and twenty-three for one from us. I know. I'm sorry. Once it's in the bank, you can only get bank rates."

"There goes sixty thousand pesos, then. Easy come, easy go. What's new in the financial world?"

We chewed the rag for a while. All we had to talk about was the ambassador's party, so we kicked it around until it wore out, and then it was time for the bank to take its mid-day *siesta*. I asked Idaho to go to lunch with me.

She looked me over carefully.

I said, "I'm a respectable business man. All I want to

do is discuss possible ways and means of salvaging those sixty thousand pesos. For your professional advice, I'll let you pick the restaurant and the lunch."

"You don't look like a respectable business man to me."

"What do I look like?"

"I'm not sure." She frowned. "Whatever it is, it isn't respectable. I'll meet you outside the side door in fifteen minutes. Over there."

It was nearer half an hour before she showed up. I didn't mind waiting. The sun was warm in the street, and I had begun to develop an idea. By the time she came through the side door and took my arm, the idea had jelled.

We walked arm in arm up Calle Bandera in the warm sunlight.

So far, all I have said about Idaho Farrell is that she was friendly and had a snub nose. About the rest of her, it will do to say that she was small, and that practically every man we passed on the street either sucked in his breath as we went by or muttered *"¡Ay!"* They do that in Chile. They do it all over South America, so I'm not picking on one country. The favorite South American outdoor sport is tossing *piropos*—compliments, you might call them—at the girls. A good-looking woman walking alone comes in for a running stream of cracks like *"¡Qué guapa!"* or *"¡Dichoso el esposo!"* or *"¡Lindíssima!"* or *"¡Dios mío, préstame la luz de los ojos para encender mi cigarrillo!"* "Lend me the light of your eyes to light my cigarette" is one of the floweriest.

Usually they are shorter and closer to the point. To be fair about it, most of the time the *piropos* are really intended as compliments, even when they are rough, and the girls expect them. If the clerk at the post office window, for example, tells a nice-looking customer that she is the flossiest piece of goods to have bought a stamp from him during his entire governmental career, she doesn't slug him. She says, Thank you very much. Of course an accompanied woman doesn't get so much of it, but she gets enough.

Idaho got more than enough, from my viewpoint. I was conditioned by Mexico City, where the attitude toward females, particularly *gringas,* isn't complimentary. Idaho must have felt my forearm tighten.

She patted my wrist.

"Don't let it get you, mister. It doesn't bother me."

"It bothers me."

"What can you do about it? Hit somebody?"

"That might help."

"It would help you to go to jail. Have you ever been in Buenos Aires?"

"Yes."

"Do you know what they do there?"

"No."

"They pinch. You can tell how popular you are by counting your black and blue spots when you get home. And if you turn around and slap them, they're insulted because you misunderstood an admiring gesture." She rubbed the place where I had spilled champagne at the embassy party. "I was two years in Argentina. Most of the time I couldn't sit down."

I had to laugh with her. We reached the restaurant she was taking me to before anybody hurt my feelings again.

The lunch was good. We ate lobster, the great big babies that come from Juan Fernández, until our eyes stuck out. Idaho said the big pincer claws made her wince, thinking of Buenos Aires. She was a good two-fisted eater, and she either didn't care what happened to her figure or knew it was too good to worry about. When we had tucked away all the groceries we could hold, she sighed guiltily.

"I'm afraid I embezzled a good meal, mister. There isn't anything you can do about your sixty thousand pesos. I'd like to help you, but the government . . ."

"Forget the pesos. I've got a better idea for you and me."

She made a face that said, "Oh-oh!"

"Strictly business. First, let me tell you why I'm here, so you'll understand what I'm talking about."

I told her all there was to tell about the job, from soup to nuts. I spelled everything out for her, told her my guesses, explained my hunches, showed her Adams' cables and the Ruano affidavits, then my passport and the license I held from the Mexican government, so she would know I was coming clean.

"I'm stuck now," I said. "I've got a strong hunch that they are selling me a turkey. I don't know what it is or what to do about it. I'd be satisfied if I could open Parker's grave and look at his teeth, but I'm pretty sure his brother won't stand for it. It may be because he doesn't want to have the body disturbed, as he says, or it may be for some other reason. I've got to see a lawyer before I'll know what to do about that end of it."

"I can tell you the answer as well as a lawyer could," Idaho said. "You can't open a grave without permission from the family or an order from the police. The police won't give you an order without something tangible to go on."

"I haven't anything tangible to go on. That's why I'm stuck."

She nodded at Adams' cablegrams, which were lying on the table.

"Have you told don Rodolfo that the affidavits aren't enough?"

"Not yet. I'm going to. I'm going to ask him to open his brother's grave. I expect him to turn me down."

"Then what?"

"Then I'll have to nose around and dig up something to use to put pressure on him. That's where you come in."

She didn't say anything.

"Here's the proposition. There was something funny about Roberto's death. Rodolfo inherited a big chunk of valuable family property when he died. You told me that Rodolfo banks with you, and he told me he gave his brother money to buy a *fundo* near Melipilla, the Hacienda Quilpué—money which he had held in trust while Roberto was away. Your bank will have a record of their financial transactions. I want . . . "

"You don't have to say any more. I can't do it."

"Let me finish. You can turn me down afterward. I'm not a crook or a blackmailer. I've told you exactly where I stand and why I need the information. Anything you give me will be used only to determine if a crime has been committed. And I'll pay a hundred dollars American for whatever you can get, whether it helps or not."

"What kind of a crime do you think was committed?"

"Murder, maybe."

"Murder?"

"Maybe. I don't know. A man who has enjoyed complete control of a lot of money for twenty years has a good motive for bumping off anybody who turns up to take it away from him. The family properties were all in Roberto's name. Even if Rodolfo shared the income with him, as he says, a whole pie is bigger than half a pie."

She pushed a bread crumb across the tablecloth with her finger.

I said, "Here's a last argument. If Roberto Ruano was murdered, it isn't my job to pin down his murderer. But I have to prove that he is really dead, and to do that I've got to get enough to squeeze somebody into cooperating with me. I think I might get what I need if I knew more about their financial transactions. If I do, I'll keep it confidential. If I don't, nobody is hurt."

I waited, watching her. She was as easy to read as a newspaper headline. I knew what was going on in her head, and I liked her more because she was on the level, even if it interfered with the job.

At last she said, "I'll think about it. I'd like to help you, if I can. But I don't want any money for it."

"The money isn't mine. It's a legitimate expense."

She flushed.

"How would you show it on your expense sheet? Bribery?"

There wasn't anything to say to that.

We left the restaurant and went back to the bank, not talking, just walking along side by side while the taxi-drivers and pool-hall cowboys sucked in their breaths and muttered *"¡Ay, Dios!"* It didn't bother me, this time. She wasn't walking with me. She just happened to be going in the same direction at the same time at the same rate of speed, thinking her own thoughts.

She wouldn't make another date with me. She said she'd look me up at my hotel in a day or two to let me know her answer. I left her at the bank and went to see a lawyer with whom I had corresponded once when I was working on an embezzlement runaway.

He told me what Idaho had told me. I didn't give him any names, just asked him what my prospects were of getting a grave open without family permission. He said they were lousy, and didn't charge me anything for the information.

After that I didn't know what to do. I felt let down. Having some kind of a lead to work on is one thing, because no matter how tough the going is you can keep working at it and feel that you are getting some place. All I had was a hunch and lots of no cooperation from everybody. Even if I did get a lead from Idaho, it would be one of those strings that had to be worked backward until I found a snarl in the line that would give me a new angle. I couldn't go forward. I had run Robert R. Parker to where the trail ended—his grave.

That was a thought. If I had to work backward, I might as well start at the end of the line.

It was still early in the afternoon. I hired the coupé again and drove to Melipilla.

9

IT WAS nearly four o'clock before I got there. Stretches of the road were out, and I had to detour a couple of times, once crossing a river on a planked-over railroad bridge that scared the devil out of me while I rattled across with three inches of clearance on either side and no railing. Otherwise I didn't mind the drive. Melipilla lies to the southwest of Santiago, where they grow some of the best fruit in the world, and the orchards were just shifting over from blossom to leaves. It was pretty country.

In Melipilla I asked my way to the *juzgado* and talked to the *alcalde,* who was shooting the breeze with the judge for the municipality. They both remembered the sad case of don Roberto Ruano very well. His remains, such as they were, had been given Christian burial on his *fundo,* not far from town.

I couldn't get anything definite out of them about Roberto's general appearance. He had been *muy caballero,* keeping pretty much to himself and his *hacienda* during the few months that he had been around. They remembered that he had ridden a big black horse, which had died with him. When I showed them the fuzzy snapshot, they said it was don Roberto to the life.

He always squinted so in the sun. They would have said the same thing if I showed them a picture of Boris Karloff as the Mad Apeman, so I hadn't got anywhere.

After I had been asking questions for a while, the *alcalde* wanted to know the nature of my interest in the tragedy. I got him away from the *juez,* who looked like a pretty sharp cookie, and gave him one of my insurance-company "special representative" cards, along with a five-hundred-peso note that had stuck to it.

"A question of insurance," I said. "When a man dies in mysterious circumstances, and there is money to be paid because of his death . . . " I shrugged.

"Of course. I understand. But there was no mystery about this, *señor.* A man rides alone around his properties and meets with an accident. It has happened before."

"I am in accord. Still, would it not be possible for me to examine such documents as you may have which bear on the matter?"

"Certainly."

The documents were in a wooden filing cabinet that sported a padlock the size and shape of a flatiron. The *alcalde* opened the padlock by yanking at it, and began to burrow through papers. There was a lot of dust in the cabinet. It came up in a cloud around his head. He sneezed while he was bringing an armload of documents over to his desk.

I said, *"Salud."*

"Gracias. Let us see. This? No. This? No. This? No."

Each "this" was a bundle of papers held together by

the remains of a rubber band. They stopped looking like bundles as he pushed them aside, because the rubber bands were so old that they had dried out, falling apart at the first strain. He finally picked one bunch of papers out of the crop, blew the dust from it, and handed it to me with a sneeze that sprayed me like a garden hose.

"*Salud.*" I plucked at the rubber band that held the bundle together. It snapped back against the paper with a good pop. "Some other person has examined these documents lately?"

"No, *señor.*"

"You are certain?"

"Not in years. Who would have the interest?"

"I could not say. But observe."

I popped the rubber band for him. He got it right away.

"You are right." He took the papers from me. "But it was not with my permission. Eugenio!"

He bellowed for Eugenio until a young kid came in from another room.

Eugenio was a clerk, from the ink on his fingers. He wore shoes and had slickum on his hair. His eyes were set too close together, but they didn't miss anything. They slid over the papers in the *alcalde's* hand, looked at me, and looked at the *alcalde,* as innocent as a pair of stuffed olives.

"*¿Si, señor?*"

"Who has examined these papers lately?" The *alcalde* shook the bundle under Eugenio's nose.

"Nobody, *señor.*"

"Do not lie to me, shameless." The *alcalde* popped the rubber band at him. "I am not blind. It is a new *hule*. Who asked to see the papers in my absence?"

"Nobody, *señor*."

"Then why does a new *hule* appear on the documents?"

The *alcalde* didn't get an answer right away because the dust caught him again and he began to sneeze. I *salud*-ed him until he stopped.

"*Gracias*. Answer me, insensible brute."

"I do not know, *señor*. I am not responsible for the *archivo*."

And that was that. Eugenio didn't even get ruffled. The *alcalde* yelled insults at him until his voice gave out, and then sent him away.

"They are all pigs and liars," he told me cheerfully.

"I can not discharge them without permission from the capital, so I have to encourage them to resign from time to time. He is lying, but what can I do?"

"Nothing, clearly. Do you have a list of the documents which should be in the file?"

"Why would I keep a list when I have the documents themselves?"

He thought that was unanswerable, so I didn't bother answering. I was pretty sure that for fifty pesos more than the original bribe Eugenio would break down and tell me who it was that had beaten me to the *archivo* and told him to keep his mouth shut about it. But I didn't need to spend the money. It had to be Fito or the old man—probably Fito did the leg work—and whatever had been in the file that they didn't want me to see, it was gone for good. Or they might have decided just to run over the record to make sure it looked right before I got that far. It didn't matter much. I knew I had them worried. If I had them worried, I was on the right trail.

The *alcalde* snapped new rubber bands around the other bundles while I went through the Ruano papers. I read everything there was to read; the death certificate, an official report of death by the local *carabineros,* a statement of identification signed by the *vaquero* who had discovered the body, another statement of identification signed by Rodolfo Ruano Parker, a receipt for certain personal possessions of the dead man, also signed by Rodolfo Ruano Parker, several other papers. There was a photograph of the body, too, but it didn't help me. The buzzards had had him too long. Even his mother wouldn't have recognized what was left.

"This Rodolfo Ruano Parker who signs papers," I said. "Who is he?"

"A relative of the dead man. A brother, I believe."

"Don't you know?"

"Yes. Almost certainly a brother. Also *muy caballero,* with a beard. Very dignified."

"Did he say he was the brother?"

"I do not remember exactly what it was he said. But he was here, shortly after the body was found, and he was very helpful. He signed all the necessary papers, as you see."

"Clearly. Yet if you are not sure that he was the dead man's brother, of what value are the papers to you?"

"I do not understand, *señor*."

I spelled it out another way for him, and he still didn't see what I was driving at. When a man died, somebody had to sign papers. It was the *alcalde's* duty to see that certain receipts, certificates, statements, documents and what not, all signed by somebody, ended up in the *archivo*. When that was done, his job was finished. If the signatures on the documents turned out to be forgeries, or if the man who signed them had misrepresented himself, it was a concern of the Bureau of Identification, not the *alcalde*. His duty was to obtain the documents.

I said, *"Claro.* It was stupid of me not to understand at once. This *vaquero* who found the body and signs himself Víctor Chavarría Serra. You know him well?"

"Certainly. He works on the *fundo.* He has been *administrador* since don Roberto's death."

"For whom does he administer?"

"The present owner."

"The brother is the present owner?"

"I do not know for certain, *señor*. The land records are maintained in the capital."

That was all I could get out of him. I copied down the name signed to the statement made by the *vaquero,* now *administrador,* of the Hacienda Quilpué, asked directions, and left the *alcalde* carefully filing his goddamn documents back in their grave.

The *fundo* was about fifteen kilometers south of town, five or six kilometers off the highway on a side road that went first through a peach orchard, then by a nice-looking patch of alfalfa in a creek bottom, and past a feeding lot where cattle were tucking away green groceries to the tune of about two pounds of new beef per head per day. From the condition of the fences and the looks of the cattle, the *fundo* was paying money. Don Rodolfo hadn't suffered financially from his brother's death.

Beyond the feeding lot, the road climbed a little hill and dropped again to the *hacienda,* a group of buildings shaded by a bunch of eucalyptus trees. There was a small graveyard by the side of the road on the crest of the hill.

I stopped the car and got out to call on Roberto.

He had a pretty nice set-up. They had built him a little cave of fieldstone and cement, all for himself, at a distance from the other graves. The cave was closed by a grilled iron door. It was locked, but I could see inside. In the back wall of the cave was a single flat piece of marble closing the place where they had put his coffin. On the marble was chiseled AQUI YACE ROBERTO RUANO PARKER, the dates of his birth and death, and DESCANSE EN PAZ. The dates checked with what I knew about him. On the floor of the cave was a vase holding a fan of dusty artificial flowers. That was all.

I hung around for a while looking in through the locked grille and feeling frustrated. Bees zoomed around among the bushes that grew in the graveyard. Six feet away from me was the answer to the big question, and there was nothing I could do about it. After seeing that photograph of what the buzzards had left of Roberto, all the affidavits in the world couldn't convince me that he was Robert R. Parker until I had looked at his teeth, whether the people who swore to the affidavits were on the level or not.

I was still standing there in front of the cave when I heard a horse coming up the road at a fast canter. I walked back toward the car. The guy on the horse got there just as I reached the gate of the graveyard. He pulled up so that his horse blocked my way out.

The horse was a big bay stallion, weighed down with a lot of flashy silver-mounted leather. The man in the saddle was about my age, dark, and had Indian blood in him. He was good-looking, in a nasty sort of way. His sideburns came down to a point just above the corners of a hard mouth. He wore tight *charro* pants, silver spurs, a silver belt buckle, and a silver-mounted holster holding a big hunk of artillery. He and the horse together would melt down at about two hundred dollars worth of bullion.

I said, *"Buenas tardes."*

"What are you doing here?"

"I look for a Señor Víctor Chavarría Serra."

He jerked his head at the graveyard.

"You expect to find him there?"

"I stopped to call on an old friend."

"So? Who is your old friend?"

"Don Roberto Ruano Parker."

The stallion skittered, kicking up dust. I put my hand on its fore-shoulder and leaned my weight on it until he gave way and I could get through the gate.

"Can you tell me where to find Señor Chavarría?" I said.

Sideburns didn't answer for a minute. Finally he said curtly, "I am Víctor Chavarría. What is your business with me?"

"My name is Colby. Don Rodolfo Ruano informed me that I would find the grave of his brother here on the *fundo*. I have interest in his death. I was told that you discovered the body."

"Yes."

"What were the circumstances of his death?"

Sideburns wanted to tell me to go to hell. I could see it in his tight mouth. He was going to tell me to go to hell sooner or later, but I thought I might get something out of him first.

He said grudgingly, "He fell from his horse."

"You have no idea what caused the fall?"

"An accident, clearly. What is your connection with him?"

"There was insurance paid. How was the body identified?"

"Don Rodolfo knew him well. I knew him well. Others on the *fundo* knew him well."

"I know. I asked how he was identified, not by whom. From the picture of the body, there was little left after the buzzards finished with him."

"The buzzards did not eat his rings nor his clothing."

Víctor's spurs jingled. The stallion moved forward, so I
had to back away. "If you talked to don Rodolfo, you
could have learned all this from him."

"I have to confirm the facts."

The stallion was crowding me over toward the car. I
could have had fun hauling Víctor out of the saddle and
wrapping him around a fence post, but there was the
gun to think about. And he was in his own backyard.

"I am told that you are *administrador* for the *fundo*."
I got my feet out of the way of the horse's hooves and
tried to pretend I didn't see Víctor using his spurs. "Don
Rodolfo is now the owner of the property?"

"You are free to ask him."

He had me backed up against the car by then. The
damn horse practically had its arms around me. There
was nothing for me to do but open the car door and
climb in.

"One more question, *caballero*," I said. "When the
body was found . . ."

"*Véte.*"

He put his hand on his gun.

I almost jumped out of the car again, gun or no gun.
Véte means Beat it. So does *vaya,* but *véte* is the form
you use with dogs, children, bums and very good
friends. Saying *véte* to a man is like calling him a son of
a bitch. If you know him well it's a joke, and if you don't
know him well it isn't funny at all.

I started the motor of the coupé. He still had his
hand on the artillery.

"Do you speak English, *señor*?"

"No. *Véte.*"

"Too bad. Before I get through with this job, I am going to haul you off that horse and bust you right in the nose. That," I said, switching back to Spanish, "means *hasta la vista. Adiós.*"

I let in the clutch and took off in second gear, leaving a nice cloud of dust in his face.

There was plenty of room for a turn near the *hacienda,* but I kept on going. As long as I was on private property, he might be able to get away with something with that big rod of his, and I didn't want to take any chances after kicking dirt in his face. I had known gun-happy guys before.

The road kept on going over the hills, past a lot of good grazing land where more fat beef cattle were putting on weight, until it came out on another highway about twenty kilometers toward the east. I didn't pass any other *haciendas* on the way. It was easy to see that the Hacienda Quilpué covered a lot of landscape. I sure wished I knew whether a lousy *vaquero* got to be *administrador* of a hunk of property like that because he was a good man or because he knew something about something.

10

I HAD a short but unpleasant session with don Rodolfo the next afternoon.

When the maid let me into the museum on Avenida O'Higgins, she said that don Rodolfo was in the *patio*. I knew my way around by then, so I told her she needn't bother to come with me.

Don Rodolfo was painting a portrait of doña María. He had an easel set up on the grass. She was sitting under the tree where the love birds bellyached in their cage. I stood in the archway leading from the house and watched them for a minute.

Don Rodolfo had his back to me. Doña María sat facing him, her hands folded in her dumpy lap, a *mantilla* over her hair, and an expression on her face that would have driven any other painter off his trolley. I don't know how to describe it. It was peace and contentment and affection and happiness and deep understanding all rolled up in one. It went with her old face the way beauty goes with a young face. While I watched her, don Rodolfo said something I didn't catch. She smiled and answered, *"Querido,"* just the one word— sweetheart, lover, beloved, however you want to translate it. He chuckled as he put a brush between his teeth. I felt as if I had wandered into their bedroom.

Doña María finally noticed me standing in the archway. Her expression changed to something more appropriate for strangers. She spoke to don Rodolfo, who turned around, saw me, put his brushes in their holder, and stood up. I came down into the *patio*.

"Excuse me if I do not shake your hand, Señor Colby," he said. "Mine is covered with paint. Please sit down."

"I will disturb you only a moment, don Rodolfo."

I went over to shake hands with doña María, which is good *chileno* etiquette. She was all set to ring the bell and order me an eight-course tea. I told her I had little time, and that if she were to tempt me again with the cooking of her kitchen I would not be able to drag myself away. It was the kind of thing you say.

Don Rodolfo waited for me to get at it. I took Adams' second cablegram out of my pocket and handed it to him. He looked at it only long enough to see that it was in English.

"I do not read English. I am sorry."

"It says my client regrets that he will need more than the affidavits."

Nobody took it from there. Doña María looked at don Rodolfo. He looked at the cablegram. I looked at the paint on his fingers, and felt like a rat.

Don Rodolfo sighed.

"Will you excuse us, please?"

He bowed from the hips to doña María. She nodded. I bowed as he had done, mumbled something, and followed him out of the *patio*. Doña María stayed as she was, her hands folded as they had been when I arrived, still in the pose he had been painting. He would have had no trouble catching her expression then. Her face was empty, drained of life.

We went into the small *sala*. Don Rodolfo gave me back the cablegram.

"What is it you wish?"

"An authority to open your brother's grave."

His mouth tightened. He said, "I regret it deeply. I cannot give you that."

"Why not?"

"We feel very strongly about such things here in Chile, Señor Colby. The words 'Rest in peace' are cut on my brother's gravestone. I will not desecrate it."

"It is very important to my client . . ."

"You speak of a matter of properties, of money." His voice was still under control, but it had an edge. "Please do not say that my brother's final rest is less important than a certain number of dollars."

"I did not mean to say that. I understand your feeling, and I regret that my position forces me to ask you this. I have no choice but to determine to my client's satisfaction—to the satisfaction of the California courts—that the man who called himself Robert Parker is truly dead."

"Will your courts not accept a death certificate, if I obtain one for you?"

"A death certificate for Roberto Ruano, the *chileno,* is not evidence of the death of Robert Parker, who called himself a United States citizen. Your affidavits that Robert Parker and Roberto Ruano are the same person have already been found inadequate."

He didn't say anything. I thought of doña María sitting in the *patio,* her hands folded, waiting. It made me mad—partly at myself, and partly because the old man was forcing me into a position where I might have to do something that would wipe that look off her face for good. I said, "If you will not help me, I must do what I can without your help. I would not like to repay your hospitality by bringing trouble to you and your family."

He lifted his head, looking down his nose at me.

"You expect to bring trouble to us?"

"I hope there is no trouble to bring you, don Rodolfo."

That ended the interview. We knew where we stood. He took me to the door. I asked him to convey my *saludes* to doña María, he said his house was mine, we shook hands. It was like getting ready to come out fighting when the bell rang.

I spent the rest of the afternoon sitting in the park, thinking. When I got back to the hotel, there were two messages for me. Miss Farrell had telephoned to say that she would be at the hotel at six o'clock. Señorita María Teresa Ruano had telephoned to say that she urgently wished to speak to Mr. Colby and would take the liberty of stopping by the hotel at seven in the hope of finding him there at that time.

Popular fellow, I thought. Girls, girls, girls.

Idaho was on time, six o'clock *en punto.* The rules at

the Carrera weren't too strict, from some of the goings-on I had seen around the joint, but I gave the head bellhop a few pesos, to make sure, and asked him to send the first lady up to my room. When she knocked at the door, the elevator boy was still hanging out of his cage down the hall, gawking at her.

"You have an admirer," I said to Idaho. "Come in."

"Who is it?"

"The elevator boy."

"Oh, him."

She turned around and whistled a wolf-call at him. He jerked his head back faster than a rabbit popping into its hole. The elevator gate slammed.

Idaho came in and looked around. It was just another hotel bedroom. I said, "I thought we could talk better here than downstairs, if we have anything to talk about. If we haven't, we'll go somewhere else and I'll buy you a drink. Sit down and relax."

"I'll sit down. I don't know whether I can relax or not."

She sat down. I sat down.

It took her quite a while to get started. After she had fidgeted for a few minutes, talking about other things, she said, "I don't feel entirely happy about this. I've brought you some information. It isn't much, but I couldn't have got it except for my position at the bank, and I don't like feeling the way I do about it. I wish I felt more certain that I wasn't—betraying somebody."

"I didn't hold anything out on you when I told you why I was here, Idaho. If Robert Parker is dead and buried, I want to prove it and go home. That's my only interest. If I were the police, I'd requisition all the information the bank has. I'm not the police and I have to get information other ways. I'm sorry if it makes you feel bad."

"Oh, I *know* you're all right. I wouldn't be here if I didn't. It's just . . ."

She shook her head, hauling a sheaf of papers out of her bag.

"Here."

The top papers were transcripts of the bank's accounts with Rodolfo Ruano for five years, and a transcript of an account with Roberto Ruano that ran for less than a year. I studied them separately, then together, until I got a kind of picture out of them.

Both accounts had been opened at about the time I figured Parker hit Chile. His account—Roberto's—started off with a lump of two and a half million pesos, about a hundred thousand dollars at the pegged exchange rate. At the same time, Rodolfo opened up with a million odd pesos and some centavos. There were periodic big deposits in Roberto's account, usually flat amounts like a hundred thousand pesos or a hundred and fifty thousand pesos, and smaller deposits in Rodolfo's account. The biggest withdrawals in either account were a charge of nearly two million pesos against Roberto, about three months after the account was opened, and an eight-hundred-thousand-peso chunk a few days later that almost cleaned him out. The account had been built back up to about five hundred thousand pesos right away, and stayed more or less at that level until it was closed out. The closing charge matched a simultaneous deposit in Rodolfo's account.

I said, "The two million looks like the purchase price of Roberto's *fundo*. What did he get for the eight hundred thousand?"

"Their house on the Avenida O'Higgins. The bank handled both transactions."

"Why would Roberto buy a house for Rodolfo?"

"He bought it in his own name. Rodolfo inherited it."

"Where did Rodolfo live before he inherited such a nice shack?"

"Antofagasta, I think. Most of the family money comes from there, through the Banco Anglo-Sudamerica."

I looked up.

"They aren't old-time residents here?"

"Not in Santiago."

"When did they come here?"

"About the time the accounts were opened, I think. They were here before I was."

That was interesting. I had got the idea, somehow, that don Rodolfo was one of the capital's founding fathers. Terry had told me that the family came from Bolivia, originally, but I had imagined the trek as something that had brought them to Santiago a long time back. If don Rodolfo had moved to Santiago from another part of Chile just about the time his brother returned from the dead, it might be worthwhile looking into the reason for the move.

This was just an idea kicking around in my head

while I studied the other papers Idaho had brought. Besides the account transcripts, there were scratch-paper summaries of various transactions in which the bank had acted for one or the other of the Ruanos; the purchase of the *fundo,* the purchase of the house on Avenida O'Higgins, the handling of Roberto's estate after his death. The record was as clear as any record can be that is only a bunch of figures on paper. If figures didn't lie—and I knew they could be made to lie—Roberto had moved into a lot of money on his return to Chile. He had bought a valuable house. He had bought an even more valuable *fundo.* He had died with these and at least half a million pesos in hard cash. Rodolfo had inherited the works.

I said, "Did you ever see a copy of the will, Idaho?"

"No. But there's a summary of it in the bank's file."

"Everything went to Rodolfo?"

"Yes."

"Rodolfo had plenty of reason to murder him, if he was murdered."

She looked sick. I said, "I'm just thinking out loud. Forget it."

I wanted to study the notes again when I had more time, so I asked Idaho if I could keep them. She said yes. Then I asked her if she would consider honoring me with her company on a tour of the town hot spots. She had a date that night and the next one, but she would be free after that. I said I would probably be going out of town for a couple of days before then. Could we leave it open until I got back?

That was all right with her. We went down to the hotel *cantina* and had a lemonade.

She was certainly a nice kid. I don't mean only in the way that made waiters and bellhops stare at her, either. As soon as she loosened up and got her mind off what she had done to the dear old bank, she was a lot of fun. She wasn't an intellectual heavyweight—or maybe she was smart enough to act dumber than she had to—but she had read a book now and then and knew what was going on in the world. She was good company. Pretty soon I even found myself telling her about me, which is a sure sign. At seven o'clock, when she had to go, I hated to see her leave. But Terry Ruano would be coming soon.

As a matter of fact, we bumped smack into Terry when I walked with Idaho out to the lobby. Terry dripped sable instead of mink, this time. She had more money on her back than they give away in two drawings of the Mexican National Lottery. It wasn't overdone. She just looked natural that way, like a diamond looks more natural set in platinum than in a piece of cheese. When Idaho saw her coming toward us, she said, "I wish I looked like that."

It was good honest envy, nothing else. I said, "You'll do the way you are," and then, "Hello, Terry. Do you know Miss Farrell? Miss Ruano."

"I've seen Miss Ruano at the bank, many times," Idaho said. "How do you do?"

"How do you do?"

There are ways and ways of saying it. Idaho's was

one way. Terry's was the way that means, Who cares? She wasn't nasty about it. She just didn't give a damn one way or the other how Idaho did. Idaho caught it as well as I did.

She said, "Well, good night. Have a good trip, Mr. Colby."

"I'd better call you a taxi. Terry, will you mind . . . ?"

"It's all right," Idaho said. "The doorman will do it."

She smiled at me, smiled at Terry, and walked away. The elevator starter's head and a couple of others turned as she passed.

Terry said, "I want to talk with you, Ahl. Where can we go?"

"Where do you want to go?"

"Any place. San Cristóbal again?"

"It got a little chilly there the other night."

She knew what I meant. She said, "I'm sorry. It was—I came tonight to explain—to apologize. Please, can't we go?"

"Your wish is my command."

I said it in Spanish, laying it on thick because I didn't like the way she had treated Idaho. She took it seriously.

"*Gracias, caballero.* If it were only true."

There was about forty feet of shiny black Packard parked outside the hotel. It pulled up in front of us before I could do anything about a taxi. I opened the door for Terry and climbed in after her. She told the chauffeur where to go.

The casino at the top of the *cerro* blared with music,

just as it had done before. The lights of the city from the terrace outside the casino looked the same, the garden on top of the hill smelled the same. Terry wore the same perfume, everything was just the same as it had been the first time—with the one difference. That was Terry.

She gave me the business. It wasn't crude or unlady-like, but it was the business just the same. She was good at it. We had a drink before dinner. She looked at me over the top of her glass, said *"salud"* in a throaty whisper, and dropped her eyelashes. During dinner she watched me and sighed—just once. When we danced, she put her head on my chest and dreamed, letting her molasses-taffy hair tickle my nose. She let me hold her hand going back to the table, and smiled at me over her shoulder when I held her chair.

It sounds bald, the way I am putting it down, but it wasn't bald. And although I knew it was an act, I still couldn't get mad because a girl who looked like a beautiful Russian spy and probably wore real diamond clips on her garters wanted to make me think she was crazy about me.

Once I found myself wondering how she would react if I said, "What are we waiting for, sugar? Let's go back to the hotel and go to bed." It made me laugh.

She said, "What are you laughing about, Ahl?"

"An old joke I remembered."

"Tell me."

"You wouldn't think it was funny."

"Tell me anyway. Please."

The "please" could have been used to candy an apple.

I said, "We didn't come here to tell jokes, did we?"

"No."

"What did we come here for?"

She hesitated.

"I came to ask you a favor."

"What?"

"Take the papers which we made for you, and go home."

"I can't. I'm sorry."

"Why must you be so stubborn?" There were angry lights in her eyes. "What more do you want here? We have given you all you need to prove what you came here to prove. My uncle is in his grave. Nothing can be served . . ."

"Nothing can be served by going over the same ground with you and your father and your brother, Terry. You've been talking to your father, so you know what I have to do. The affidavits are not enough, that's all. A hundred affidavits wouldn't convince me until I get the answers to some of the questions I've asked. If your uncle is dead and buried, as you say, the answers should be simple, direct and honest. I haven't got an honest answer from you to any of my questions. Why? What are you hiding?"

She said in a low voice, "I will try to answer the questions you asked the other night, if you will ask them again."

"All right. But I have another to ask, first. Will you try to persuade your father to give me authority to open your uncle's grave?"

She was a long time answering.

"You asked Fito that," she said.

"He said no. Your father told me once that he would consider it as a last resort. When I asked him today, he refused flatly."

"He would not consent, I am sure. He feels very strongly about such things."

"What is your answer?"

She shook her head unhappily.

"I can not persuade my father to do anything he does not want to do. It is useless to ask me that question, Ahl."

I stood up.

"It's useless to ask you anything. Let's go."

She caught my hand.

"No! No! I want to help you! I don't want anything bad to happen, Ahl! Please believe me! Let me answer your questions as well as I can, so you will be satisfied and go home. Please!"

She was a damn good actress. The tears were messing up her makeup, and she clung to my hand with both of hers. Other people on the terrace were watching us. I could either stand there like a wife-beater caught in the act, or drag her out of her chair, or sit down. I sat down.

"All right. Fix your face, will you?"

She fixed her face. I watched the moving lights of traffic in the city below. When we were back on an even keel once more, I said, "Why did your uncle carry the picture of Fito with him?"

"He had both pictures—one of me and one of Fito. My

mother gave them to him before he went away. He lost the one of Fito. I don't know where you found it . . ."

"In an automobile he sold in Mexico City. What about the other one?"

"It was among his things when he died. It came to my father as part of the estate."

"Your father was the only heir?"

"Yes. My uncle had no other relatives."

"Your uncle must have been very fond of his niece and nephew to carry their pictures so faithfully."

"He had no children of his own. *Chilenos* are very sentimental about their families Even I carry a picture of my grandmother in a locket."

It was a possible explanation, although I wasn't sold on it. I tried the next question.

"Why did you tell me you had never heard of Robert Ruíz Parker, when we first met, and then ask me to your home so your father could tell me all about him?"

"We had concealed his identity for so long that I— lied—automatically. Later, when I spoke to Fito, he thought it would be wiser to find out why you were here, and what you wanted. My father made the decision to tell you what he did."

"Did you know why your uncle was so anxious to hide?"

"I knew that he had lived an unhappy life in the States, and wanted to escape it."

"Did you know that he deserted his wife?"

She nodded miserably. The questions were hurting her, or her family pride, or something, but she didn't try to duck them. I said, "Do you remember what the last question was that I asked you before?"

She nodded again, keeping her eyes down.

"I'm not going to ask it this time. It wasn't fair, and it has nothing to do with the job. But I'd like to ask one other question before I stop."

I waited so long that she looked up. I said, "What will you do when I tell you that I'm going to Antofagasta tomorrow to look into the history of the Ruano family there?"

It was a good hit, for a shot in the dark. Her face turned white. I thought she was going to faint. Before I could move, she had snapped out of it.

I handed her a glass of water, and a napkin to wipe her mouth. Her hand was as cold as a dead man's when it touched mine.

She said, "Why do you want to go to Antofagasta?"

She was trying hard to make it sound as if she didn't care much what the answer was.

"Didn't your family live there at one time?"

"Yes. But what do you expect to learn?"

"I don't know."

"You will only waste your time there, Ahl."

"I might as well waste it there as here."

She didn't know what to say. She wanted to try to persuade me not to go, and she was afraid to let me see how important it was to her. I had scared her badly. I didn't enjoy scaring her, and I had learned what I wanted to learn. I made a noise at a *mesero* who had come out on the terrace.

He brought me the check. I paid it while Terry was fixing her face for the second time.

I said, "Do you want to dance again, or shall we go?"

"I think we had better go."

We didn't talk any more until we were driving across the bridge that crossed the river below the *cerro*. I said, "Shall I take you home, or do you want to drop me at the hotel?"

"I'll let you off at the hotel"

She leaned over to speak to the driver. There was a curtain that pulled down between his seat and ours. After she had told him to stop at the Carrera, she pulled the curtain down.

"Ahl."

It was almost a whisper.

"What?"

"You didn't ask me that one question, but I'll answer it. I don't want anything bad to happen to my father or my family. I don't want anything bad to happen to you. If you go on with this thing, something bad will happen either to them or to you. I—I couldn't stand it. Please give it up."

She had a pretty authentic catch in her voice. There was enough light in the car for me to see that her eyes were shiny, too. So were her lips, shiny and red and soft and tasting like raspberry when I put my arms around her warm body inside the sable coat and kissed her. Only a very rude fellow would have failed to cooperate at that point, and I am not a rude fellow. Besides, I had never kissed anybody who owned a sable coat and a mink coat at the same time.

The kiss lasted two or three blocks. I came up for air as we stopped in front of the hotel.

"Good night," I said, breathing like an old pump. "I'll call you when I get back from Antofagasta."

I was out of the car before she could say anything. The Packard pulled away.

When I asked for my key at the desk, the clerk reached under the counter and handed me a Kleenex, without a word or a smile. I wiped my mouth, reminding myself to give him either a good tip or a good boot in the pants when I left the hotel.

11

ANTOFAGASTA isn't a bad place after you get there. It's an old city, and a lot of people put a lot of time into planting parks and trees to take the curse off what they had to start with, which wasn't much. The town lies on the coastal edge of the northern desert, where the nitrates come from. Behind the town, steep dirt hills shove up from the coast to a flat plain stretching away toward the Andes. The hills look like something left there by an excavator; nothing grows on them, not a scrubby bush or a cactus plant, only big whitewash letters painted on the dirt that say Smoke This and Drink That and Use Something Else for bad breath. Since it practically never rains in that part of the world, the signs stay on the side of the hill until somebody paints something else equally ugly over them. The best thing to do in Antofagasta is to keep looking seaward, if you can manage it.

I came into town on a LAN plane that dumped me off at the airport an hour after sunup. I hadn't slept during the flight, so I hired a horse-drawn something that called itself a victoria and let it take me to the Hotel Maury, where I pounded my ear for a couple of hours. After a bath and a pretty good lunch, I felt more like tackling the job.

First I tried the Banco Anglo-Sudamerica.

They didn't throw me out on my ear, although the thought was there. I don't know whether they had been tipped off or were only acting like a bank, but the answer was the same either way. They wouldn't even agree with me when I said it was a nice day. Every time I tried to ask a question, they wanted to know what business it was of mine. I couldn't answer that one satisfactorily, so I moved on to the office of the local *camera de comercio*.

Don Rodolfo had told me that the family money came from nitrates. I told the chamber of commerce fellow that I represented a couple of million American dollars looking for a sound investment, not including copper or guano. That left nitrates.

He gave me a list of companies exploiting the nitrate beds. It was pretty long, and the name of Ruano didn't show on it, so I said of course I would only be interested in dealing with an organization in which ownership was concentrated in a few hands, as I did not want to fritter away my youth and beauty running down minority interests. That cut the list way down. After a little more jockeying, I had the *camera de comercio* offering me the Compañía Nitrata de Calama, S.A., as if it had been their own idea from the start. The Compañía Nitrata de Calama, S.A., was a sound, old-time corporation wholly owned by *el heredero de don Roberto Ruano Parker*. I would find the office of the heir on Calle Prat.

I found the office all right. It was one room at the

end of a dark passageway in an old building that smelled like a chicken coop. The office was half as big and twice as dark as the inside of a steamer trunk. It held a desk, one chair, a lot of ledgers, and a little old wizened *chileno* who was writing something in one of the ledgers with a scratchy pen.

I said, *"Buenos días"* from the doorway. There wasn't room for me inside.

The old guy peered up at me.

"This is the office of the heir of don Roberto Ruano Parker?"

"It might be so."

"I am interested in nitrate properties. I should like to make an offer to the heir for his holdings."

"So?"

"You are authorized to act for the heir?"

"To an extent."

"To such an extent that you could acquaint me with the nature of the holdings?"

"Possibly."

I'll bet he thought up fifty different ways of saying "maybe" before I gave up. My idea was to work my way in with the bluff about nitrate properties, and then skillfully steer him around until he was telling me the life history of the Ruanos. He steered about as easily as a fire hydrant. He never said yes, he never said no, and he never let a dribble of information sneak away from him. It finally got under my skin.

I said, "You have undoubtedly heard of the proverb concerning the ass which died in his master's service and was rewarded by having his hide made into a whip with which to lash his successor?"

"Perhaps."

"There is another proverb which attributes wisdom to the man who sells what he has to sell when the market is available. It would apply to asses as well."

His upper lip lifted enough to show his teeth. It was as close as he ever came to a smile.

"There is also a third, *señor*: Into a closed mouth, no flies enter. Even an ass can appreciate the beauty of the saying."

I tipped my hat, bowed, and turned away, leaving him there in his hole with the faint grin on his wrinkled old puss.

I felt pretty low when I wandered back to the hotel.

It had been a mistake to let Terry know I was coming to Antofagasta. They had had plenty of time to dam up all the available sources of information against me. As long as they knew where I was and what I was doing, I was wasting my time.

I ate a terrible dinner at the hotel. Afterward I strolled through the lobby to see if I could find a magazine or something to help me pass the time before I cried myself to sleep.

There was an announcement board in the hotel lobby. It was one of those things with a slotted black background in which the hotel management sticks white metal letters to spell out whatever is cooking locally that might interest the hotel guests. The Club Rotario de Antofagasta was having a meeting at nine-thirty. That left me cold. So did the local movie, and a dance at the Automobile Club. What caught my eye was an announcement that hotel guests might apply at the desk for guest cards making available to them the privileges of the British Club and the Club Unión.

I almost broke a leg getting over to the desk. One of the cards don Rodolfo had given me was to the Club Unión in Santiago. In Chile, the Club Unión is like the Lion's Club, or better yet, the Republican Party. You may move around from place to place, but you go right on belonging, wherever you are. If don Rodolfo was a club member in Santiago, he damn near had to have been one in Antofagasta when he lived there. And if I couldn't find at least one old-timer at the club who had known the Ruano boys, I would turn in my suit to the coach.

It was as easy as dropping an egg. At the club I showed the boy at the desk the guest card from the hotel and the corner of a bill, and asked him if a don Rodolfo Ruano had been a member of the club up until four or five years before. He said yes, without hesitation. I asked him if a don Roberto Ruano had also been a member of the club many years earlier, say twenty years back. He couldn't answer that offhand, but he looked through the records and came up with another yes. Don Roberto Ruano had been dropped for non-payment of dues eighteen years before.

"One more thing." I wadded up the bill so he could take it without anybody seeing him break the club rules. "Is there, perhaps, someone in the club at the moment who has been a member for more than twenty years? Or can you tell me . . . ?"

"Don Guillermo Unfres has been a member of the club for forty years. You will find him in the *cantina*."

"Unfres?" It didn't sound like any Latin name I had ever heard before.

"Unfres. An old one, with a colored nose."

He wasn't fooling about the colored nose, either. It looked like the port light on a steamboat when I found the old boy sitting alone at a table in the bar, peering at himself in a gin rickey. There were other men in the bar, but they were in tight knots as far as they could get from the Nose, facing away. It was the double wing-back formation you use to keep the club bore from grabbing your lapel.

I said, "Señor Unfres?"

"Humphreys." He had a thin, scratchy voice. "Willie Humphreys. Glad to see you again, son. Siddown."

I sat down.

"I don't think you've seen me before, Mr. Humphreys. My name . . ."

"Call me Willie, son. Everybody calls me Willie."

"O.K., Willie. My name is Al Colby. I heard you were an old-timer here. I want to know something about the club members."

"I was standing on the curb when the club was built," Willie said. "I spit on the cornerstone when they were putting it down. What do you want to know?"

He didn't say spit, either, but I have to clean up his conversation. He was a bawdy old bastard. He must

have been eighty, at least, but whenever his conversation wandered away from the point—and it wandered
a lot—he always ended up talking about the girls and
related subjects. He was pretty funny to listen to, once.
I suppose the other club members had heard him gab so
often that they had to shut him out in self-defense. That
made me very popular with him as a listener.

Like a lot of people when they get that old, his
memory was better for things that had happened a long
time ago than remembering what he had eaten for
lunch. And he telescoped once in a while, so that
something that had happened to him fifty years before
would lead on to something else that happened forty
years later, all in the same sentence. But I learned that
he had come to Chile from the States as a kid, not long
after the war in which Chile yanked the coastal nitrate
fields away from Bolivia and cut her off from the
Pacific. It had been a catch-as-catch-can scramble for
the loot in those days, Bolivian land titles against
Chilean land titles, another gold-rush where anybody
with a gun to hold his claim and a mule-drawn scraper
to operate it could skim a fortune in nitrate right off the
ground. Willie had made his claim stick and milked his
pile out of it.

"Those were the days, son," he said. "Rough, tough
and rambunctious. Work all day, drink all night, and
nothing to do on Sundays but play billiards and guess-
what."

He winked at me. A *mesero* came by. I ordered a
beer and another gin rickey.

"Did you ever know a man named Roberto Ruano, Willie?"

"Sure. Fine boy. Operated a property near me up by Calama. Used to play billiards with him. "

"Here in the club?"

"Here and before the club was built. Any place there was a billiard table. The country wasn't like it is now, since this goddamn government started spending money on damn fool moving picture palaces for a bunch of goddamn *rotos*. There wasn't anything to do but play billiards, after we got too tired to guess-what. That wasn't often, though. I remember once in Bequedano . . ."

"You knew Roberto Ruano pretty well, then?"

"Like a son. Fine lad."

It was strange to be sitting there listening to him saying "Fine lad" about a man who was old enough to be my father, but I realized that he had twenty-five or thirty years head start on Roberto. That made Roberto a lad as far as he was concerned.

I said, "Remember when he left here?"

He squinted an eye at me.

"Who?"

"Roberto Ruano."

"Quite a while back, was it?"

"Nearly twenty years, I think. He may have turned up again later, but I'm thinking of the first time. At least twenty years ago, maybe longer."

Willie took the rickey the *mesero* had brought him and sucked at it.

"Live to be a hundred on this stuff," he said. "Stick to

gin and lime juice and you can't go wrong. I remember that he wasn't around for quite a spell. Had to get a new billiard partner." Willie scowled at the double wingback formation across the way. "None of these squirts know a billiard cue from the east end of a snake. Club's going to hell fast. I remember once . . ."

"Did you ever see Roberto Ruano afterward?"

"After what?"

"After he left here twenty years ago."

"Nope. Can't say that I have. Don't remember *not* seeing him again, though. If he was around the club, I probably saw him. Spend all my time here.

"That's what I'm trying to find out. Did he turn up here again after he went away?"

"After he went away where?"

I swallowed a mouthful of beer. My neck muscles were so tight they hurt. After I got them relaxed, I tried again.

"You don't remember seeing Roberto Ruano again after he left here twenty years ago. Is that right?"

"That's what I said, isn't it? Finish that slop and I'll buy you a real drink. Stick to gin and lime juice and you'll live to be a hundred."

"Gin doesn't agree with me, thanks. I'll have another beer. Do you know why Roberto Ruano left here?"

"Nope. Probably wanted to go somewhere else."

Later I checked with the boy at the desk, hoping the club records would show something more, and drew a blank. Roberto had been dropped from the club after his unpaid dues piled up for a couple of years. They had

no other record of him. All I could get out of Willie was
that he had known Roberto well in the boom days, had
played billiards and catted around with him at one time
or another, and had never heard of him again after he
disappeared twenty years before. I tried the fuzzy
snapshot on him. He said it wasn't a very good picture,
which I knew already, but it could be Roberto, all right.
He remembered once they had been helling around
Coquimbo . . .

I said, "How well did you know Rodolfo Ruano?"

"Rodolfo. Rodolfo. Which one was he?"

"The brother. He plays a good game of billiards, too."

"Oh, Rodolfo. Sure. Fine lad, fine lad. Knocked the
balls around with him many times. Haven't seen him
around lately, either."

"He's been living in Santiago for four or five years."

"Is that so? Hey, *mesero. Me muero de sed.*"

He beat his glass on the table.

The waiter brought him another rickey before he
finished dying of thirst. I got him back on the subject of
Rodolfo long enough to learn that he had known Rodolfo only around the club, long after he and Roberto had
done their helling in the rough, tough, rambunctious
days of the nitrate boom. That tied in with what don
Rodolfo had said about his brother doing all the de-
velopment work on the family properties, and I wasn't
much interested in don Rodolfo anyway. When Willie
wandered off on the subject of what a devil he and
Roberto had been with the girls in Tocopilla, I let him
talk, hoping he'd spring something about Roberto that

might help me. He didn't.

When I think back and realize how close I was then to wrapping the job up in a parcel, it makes me want to bang my head against the wall. Two or three more questions to pin the old windbag down and I would have had it. I asked a lot of questions, but they weren't the right ones. Willie wandered on through four or five more rickeys, repeating himself half the time and mixing his dates up so that I never knew whether he was talking about something that had happened before I was born or the day before yesterday. I could see why the other club members had put the freeze on him.

I got away from him about 2 A.M. I felt logy from all the beer and baloney I had absorbed, so I walked back to the hotel instead of taking a victoria.

I had to go through the Plaza Colón on the way home. It was more of a park than a plaza; grass, a few trees, statues parked here and there along the walks. One statue was a bronze lion that had been presented to the city by somebody or other for some reason. A metal plate set into the granite pedestal gave all the details of the presentation, but it was too dark for me to read even if I'd been interested. All I cared about was the pedestal, which made a good windbreak against the breeze coming in off the ocean. I stopped to light a cigarette.

The bullet went SPLAT! against the granite by my head. It was maybe an eighth of a second later before I heard the shot, and my hand was already starting up to brush at the hot lead that had stung my ear before I knew what had happened. I let go everything and dropped flat.

There wasn't another shot, but I felt too naked against that nice tombstone-colored granite to stick around. I took two corners of the statue on my hands and knees and stayed there until a couple of *carabineros* ran up and wanted to know what was going on.

As soon as my legs got steady enough to hold me up, I showed them the bullet-pock on the granite. They got out their guns and nosed around the plaza without finding anything or anybody. One of them said the guy must have been a terrible shot.

I didn't argue with him. I didn't know whether it had been a terrible shot or just a warning to pull my ears in, but I didn't want to think about it. When the *carabineros* asked my name, address, nationality, height, weight, occupation, religion, marital status and why would anybody be trying to send me to the boneyard, I told them I didn't know the answer to the last one but that if they wanted to get in touch with me at any time after the next plane left town, they could communicate with me at the Hotel Carrera in Santiago. In the meantime, would one or both of them kindly accompany me back to the Hotel Maury?

They both did. I gave them some pesos for the Widows and Orphans fund. I might be leaving widows and orphans of my own some day, if I lived long enough.

12

IN CASE anybody thinks I was scared, I was. There is something about the splat of a bullet next to your head that stays in the memory, particularly when it hits close enough to leave a blister on your ear.

Thinking about it later, I decided that it must have been a warning. There had been no need to shoot at my head while my whole body was outlined against the light-colored granite of the pedestal. I didn't overlook the possibility that the shooter might have been inexperienced, in which case the kick of an unfamiliar gun could lift the bullet several feet over its target, but an inexperienced shooter who was really anxious to pot me would have blazed away three or four times while I was scuttling around corners on my hands and knees. I was being told to watch myself.

Bearing this in mind, I left Antofagasta without asking further questions. As long as they could keep an eye on me and know what progress I was making they might decide to snooker me with another and better-placed bullet. My hide came first. Secondarily, I had decided to stop fooling around. Having bullets thrown at me in Antofagasta might not be enough to persuade the police to open a grave in Melipilla, but it was enough for me.

The Christian charity I had felt until then toward the

Ruano family was all gone. They might yet bump me off. If they did, I wanted somebody to know all the facts so that steps could be taken afterward to do something about it. I thought of going to my pal Lee in Valparaíso, but that meant putting him officially on notice of a possible perjury before a United States consular official. I wasn't ready for that yet. The only other person I could trust was Idaho Farrell.

As soon as I got into Santiago, I dropped my bag off at the hotel and went down to the bank. A sniffy young fellow in the foreign exchange department told me that Annie didn't work there any more.

"Where does she work?"

"I'm sure I couldn't say. She was discharged yesterday."

"Why?"

"I'm sure I couldn't say."

"Where can I get her address?"

"The personnel department might give it to you. I couldn't say."

The personnel department didn't want to say, either, at first. They wouldn't tell me why Idaho had been bounced, even when I pointed out that I had twenty-five hundred dollars worth of pesos in their pockets which I could easily move somewhere else, but they finally gave me her address.

It was a clean little *pensión* on the east side of town, near the river. When I got there, she was sitting in a hammock in the *patio* reading a book. Her eyes were red and puffy.

I said, "What happened?"

She went boo-hoo-hooo. I sat down in the hammock and put my arms around her. I would rather have been in a hammock with her under different circumstances, but even then it was no chore. She wept into my collar for a while before it came out.

"Th-they fired me. María Teresa must have told her father that she saw me with you, because Fito came to the bank and asked the m-manager about me and the manager found out I had been asking about the Ruano accounts and I h-had to t-tell h-him . . ."

She choked on it.

"I'm sorry, Idaho. It was my fault. I shouldn't have asked you to do it."

"I don't care. It's just that I worked for the d-damn bank so long and now they say I violated my contract. They won't pay my passage home and I can't get another j-job without a r-recommendation, and—and . . ."

She blubbered.

"You don't have to worry," I said. "It's my fault. I'll make up what you lost."

She finally quieted down, took her head off my shoulder, and wiped her nose. It—her nose—was pretty shiny by then, but she was wearing a sweater that would have kept anybody in his right mind from looking at her face anyway. I got a brilliant idea.

It wasn't entirely original. I had heard the story of the girl in the States who cashed forged checks at every bank in the country and got away with it for weeks because her dress was cut so low in front that none of the tellers who took the phony paper could tell the cops what her face looked like. I didn't have anything that crude in mind for Idaho, but any man who watched me when he could be watching her or any part of her would be crazy.

I said, "How much were you making at the bank?"

"T-ten thousand pesos a month."

That was about four hundred dollars at the pegged exchange rate. I said, "How would you like to work for me for a while?"

"You?" She was so surprised that she stopped sniffling.

"I'll pay you two hundred a month, in dollars. That's almost ten thousand pesos on the free market."

"What would I have to do?"

"Write letters when I have any, run errands, ask no questions, and look luscious."

She looked luscious and suspicious at the same time. I said, "I don't know how long the job will last, but I'll pay you a month's salary to start. It will hold you long enough to see if you can get another job. If you can't, I'll give you plane fare back to the States."

"You don't have to . . ."

"I owe you the plane fare because it was my fault that you lost your job. The salary is because I need your help."

"Writing letters?"

"Looking luscious, primarily."

She was still suspicious. I turned my head to be sure nobody was within listening distance.

"I'm going to open Parker's grave."

"But you can't!"

"I can. I have to. Somebody took a shot at me in Antofagasta yesterday. I don't know whether it was intended to hit me or not, but the next one may be. Old man Ruano has me boxed, and I don't know enough yet to threaten him. If Parker's body is in the grave, I can go home. If it isn't, I'll be able to squeeze the whole family for perjury on those affidavits they gave me, and maybe a few other things. Until I get the grave open, I'm only wasting my time and risking my neck."

"If the grave is that important, you'll be risking your neck trying to get into it."

"That's why I need you."

"What do you want me to do?"

"I'll tell you later when I've thought it out. There'll be no danger. I can cover up your part in it so that you'll be in the clear whatever happens. But I can't handle it alone, and I've got to get action before they hamstring me."

"Why don't you take the affidavits and go home? You can make them do, if you really want to."

I shook my head.

"But why? Is it because they shot at you? Are you so bitter at them . . . ?"

"I'm not bitter at them. I like them."

She couldn't understand it. I tried to explain.

"It's a job, Idaho. My business is doing odd jobs, like this one. My only stock in trade is a reputation for honest delivery. When I lose the reputation, I'm out of business. I was hired to find Parker, dead or alive, and until I can go home and say I personally am satisfied that I've done what I was hired to do, I haven't earned my money. That's all."

"And for that you're willing to risk being killed?"

"It isn't as bad as that. I won't be risking anything if you help me."

I patted her shoulder and heaved myself up out of the hammock.

"Tomorrow morning we'll take a ride in the country. Wear that skirt and sweater, and fix your hair the best way you know how. Do you have a pair of fancy shoes with high heels?"

"Yes. But if we're going to the country . . ."

"You won't be doing any walking. I want you to fix yourself up the way you would in Buenos Aires if you were getting a bonus for every black-and-blue mark."

It made her laugh. She felt a lot better when I left her than she had when I arrived, even if she didn't know what I was up to.

I bought a set of tools at a hardware store not too near the hotel. The main thing I needed was a good strong jimmy and an automobile ignition fuse. I got a couple of other things to be on the safe side. I thought for a while of getting a gun, too, but I found out that I would need a license before I could buy one, and arranging for a license would be too difficult. Besides, if I was going to be shot at again, this time it would be as a trespasser and grave robber. Shooting back would only make me a possible murderer as well. I let the gun go.

The afternoon took a long time to go by. Remembering the splat of that bullet and thinking about what I had to do the next day made me jumpy. I found myself setting traps to see if I was being tailed. There wasn't anybody in Chile who could stay on my tail if I wanted to shake him, but I was more interested in learning if I had company than getting rid of it. Nobody walked into my traps.

My second brilliant idea for the day came to me as I was passing the Panagra ticket office. I went in and bought a ticket to Mexico City. They couldn't give me a guaranteed through flight inside of forty-eight hours, because there were no earlier reservations open north of Panama. Forty-eight hours was just what I needed before I would know whether I was ready to leave or had to cancel the ticket, so I acted like a man in a hell of a sweat to get out of the country; were they sure they couldn't get me away any sooner, and would the flight leave on schedule, and so on. If I *did* have a tail on me, he'd have a satisfactory report to take home after he had followed me into the ticket office and asked a couple of questions.

With that out of the way, I did a little fancy doubling to make sure I was all alone, ending up at the LAN ticket office. They remembered me, because I had bought my ticket to Antofagasta there only two days before. I asked them if a Señor Ruano had purchased a ticket to Antofagasta at about the same time I did. I had expected to meet Señor Ruano in Antofagasta. However, I had missed him, and I was anxious to mumble mumble

mumble mumble, *por favor.*

They looked it up. Señor don Rodolfo Ruano had been on the flight which preceded mine. They could not understand how we had missed each other. Señor Ruano either still remained in Antofagasta or had returned by Panagra or some other means of transportation, as they had no record of his return by any of their planes.

It surprised me to know that don Rodolfo had followed me north himself. I had expected to learn that it was Fito. I supposed the old man had figured that pulling triggers or hiring somebody to pull triggers was business too delicate to trust to one of the kiddies. It didn't matter much. They ought to leave me alone now until it was time for my plane to take off for Mexico. By then I would either be ready to go or ready to blow the Ruanos out of the water.

It was about five o'clock when I got back to the hotel with my bundle of tools. I didn't feel jumpy any more, only tired. A *siesta* before dinner would fix me up. First I burned out the ignition fuse by jamming it slantwise into a light socket. Then I took a hot bath and lay down for a catnap.

I was out for twelve hours, as cold as if I had been hit on the head with an ax. It was getting light when I woke up. I thought it was sunset instead of sunrise, and because my watch had stopped I called the desk to ask the time. The desk said 6 A.M., good morning.

It was as good a time as any to start. First I phoned Idaho, to let her know I was coming. I didn't feel much like breakfast, but I ate some anyway, put my tools in a suitcase along with the chart of Parker's dental layout, and lugged the suitcase to the elevator. I had to push off a couple of bellhops in the lobby, and explain that I wasn't trying to jump my hotel bill, but I got the suitcase out to the street and into a taxi without letting anybody hear the tools rattle.

Idaho was waiting for me at the *pensión*. She had dug up another sweater that fit even better than the one I had seen, and the shoes were all anybody could ask for. So was her hair. She let me and the taxi-driver gawp at the get-up for a minute before she put on a long coat she was carrying and climbed into the taxi.

"I feel like a chippy," she said, still blushing. "Is it all right? Or did I overdo it?"

"It's perfect. If you don't stop traffic cold, I'll eat the spare tire on this heap. Which reminds me. I forgot to ask you if you could drive a car."

"Yes."

"Good."

"What do I have to do besides drive a car?"

"Wait awhile and I'll tell you. Here's two hundred dollars American, your first month's salary, and twenty-five hundred pesos for expense money."

She took the money without asking foolish questions. I said, "We're going to a place where they rent automobiles. They'll ask your name and address and a few other things, and make you put up a deposit. If they ask where you intend to go with the car, tell them for a drive in the country—because it's spring, or anything you like. Let them know you're alone. Get a sedan, a

Chevrolet, if they have one. If you have no choice, take whatever you can get except a green Ford coupé. I'll be waiting around the first corner to your right as you come out of the garage. Pick me up there."

I let her off a block from the garage, and then had the taxi-driver take me and my burglar kit around the corner.

It was fifteen or twenty minutes before Idaho came around the corner in a sedan. It was a Chevrolet, which only mattered to me because I knew where the fuses were on a Chevrolet without hunting for them, but at least we were starting off right. I slung my bag into the back seat and jumped in front.

"Do you know how to get to Melipilla?"

"Yes."

"That's where we're going."

While she drove, I felt under the dashboard for the fuse clips. They were pretty stiff. I sprang them a little so she could get a fuse out without busting a fingernail. Then I showed her where it was, slipped the fuse out of the clips so she could see what it looked like, and slipped it back into place before the car had time to lose speed on the dead engine.

"Now listen carefully," I said.

13

"I'LL BE ON THE FLOOR in the back seat when you drive through Melipilla," I told her. "About fifteen kilometers past the town there's a side road to the right and a sign that says 'Hacienda Quilpué.' You turn off there. Five or six kilometers farther along there's a little graveyard at the side of the road. The road goes over a hill there. If anybody is in sight when you get there keep on going. If not, slow down enough for me to jump before you get to the top of the hill. The *hacienda* is in the valley on the far side of the hill, and I want to get off before the car can be seen from there. Follow me so far?"

"Yes."

"After you get over the top of the hill, pull the fuse out of the clips I showed you and let the car coast at least a hundred yards. Put this dead fuse in the clips as soon as you can and put the good one in your purse where you can find it in a hurry. Then look helpless. If nobody shows up, stay put until I get there. If anybody, particularly a slick-looking *latino* with sideburns, comes around, your job is to keep him occupied until you hear from me. I don't care how you do it, but if it's Sideburns, as I expect, I think he fancies himself as a ladies' man. Your best bet is to get out of the car and let him look at you—without the coat. I don't think he'll want to leave after that."

"Would you like me to do a strip-tease for him? I want to be sure I'm earning my salary."

Idaho's voice wasn't cold, but it wasn't warm. I said, "I'm sorry if it sounds bald. I'm explaining the set-up so you'll know what you're doing. Tell anybody who asks that the motor simply went dead, and that you have to get back to Santiago before noon. You came this way because you thought it was a short-cut. Sideburns may know enough to find the burnt-out fuse. If he does, he probably won't be able to dig up a replacement, but he can short the connections so the motor will start. If he gets that far, tell him you smelled something burning just before the motor went dead, and make him check all the wiring. I'll probably need half an hour. It's up to you to hold him and the car there until I'm finished, anyway you like. If he does manage to get it started, don't go any farther than the *hacienda,* wait for me there, and *keep him with you.* Get it?"

She nodded, keeping her eyes on the road ahead. Her face looked stiff.

"There's one more thing. I don't expect anything to go wrong, but it could. If trouble starts, put the good fuse in place and get away as fast as you can. The road will bring you out on a highway that goes into Santiago. Nobody knows I'm with you, so if they question you later you stick to the story that you were just out for a drive. You don't know why the motor conked out or why it started again when you tried it, but you did. The shooting scared you off."

I put my foot in it good with that. Idaho's head turned quickly.

"Shooting?"

"Keep your eye on the road. I meant commotion. There'll probably be an argument, if they catch me."

"You mean you'll probably be shot, don't you?"

"I don't know. It's a chance I've got to take. I don't expect to be caught."

We were getting near Melipilla then, so I crawled over into the back seat with the burglar kit and kept my head down while the car bumped over cobblestones. Beyond the town, I poked my head up again and watched for the turn-off.

"Here it is," I said. "I'm going back into the hole now. Give me the word when you're ready to stop."

Idaho made the turn. I could hear the sound of the tires change as we hit the soft dirt of the side road. After a minute she said, "Al."

It was the first time she had ever called me that. I said, "What?"

"I'm scared. I'm shaking all over. Don't go through with it."

"There's nothing to be scared of."

I didn't tell her that my own feet were as cold as a couple of iced mackerel. I knew damn well what Sideburns would do with that big roscoe of his if he caught me robbing graves. The law would be on his side, too. I concentrated hard on the idea that I had a fool-proof scheme.

Idaho said, "Please."

"Are you backing out?"

"No. I'm afraid for you."

I wanted her to stop talking about it before my feet got any colder. I said, "You do your end of it and I'll be all right. Can you see the graveyard yet?"

"No. Yes, I see it. On the left?"

"That's it. Anybody in sight?"

"No."

"Be sure. Look all around."

"Nobody."

"Good. Say when."

Forty-five heartbeats later—I could feel them pounding in my ears—she said, "Now!" The car slowed. I grabbed my burglar kit, opened the door, and jumped.

The dust cloud covered me until I got inside the graveyard. A guard stationed behind a tombstone would have ruined me, but they hadn't got that cautious yet. I took the jimmy out of my bag and sprang the grilled gate of Parker's cave open on the first try, not even breaking the lock. My nerves didn't bother me at all, once I was busy.

Inside the cave, I closed the grille behind me and moved the fan of paper flowers out of the way. There were a couple of chisels and a maul in my bag, but I didn't need them. The mortar around the stone in the back wall of the cave was mostly sand. It came away under the sharp end of the jimmy. I had the stone out in about two minutes.

The rollers under Parker's coffin were still there. I slid the box out carefully and let one end down to the floor. The niche was just high enough so that I could leave the other end propped up on the ledge. The coffin wasn't heavy, but it was plenty heavy enough for me not to want to have to muscle it back into place in a hurry if I could help it. I jammed the headstone under the floor end to hold it on the slant.

Outside, bees droned back and forth among the bushes. I stopped to listen. Something that might have been the faint pound of hoofbeats or the loud pound of my heart thumped in my ears. I waited for a while, but the sound didn't get any louder. I thought, hold that line, Idaho.

There were eight screws in the coffin lid. I had bought one of those automatic screwdrivers that work on a ratchet arrangement, and I ran the screws out as fast as I could pump my arm up and down. When the lid hung from one screw, I took out my handkerchief, soaked it in a bottle of camphor I had in my pocket, and tied it around my face. The stuff choked me, but it might be better than what I had to look at next.

It wasn't as bad as I had expected. The buzzards had picked the bones cleaner than had been shown by the *alcalde's* photograph. What was left besides bones had turned into leather. There was enough to hold the skeleton together inside its clothes, and that was about all. It had sagged down in the coffin when I tipped it, without falling apart.

I said, "Excuse me, whatever your name is," and

reached for the dental mirror and flashlight that were in my bag. The skeleton's lower jaw fell open as I touched it.

His teeth were still there, just as they had been when he was buried. The examination took me such a short time that I wasted another few minutes trying to find some evidence that he had been murdered. One rib on the left side was shattered, but I didn't know enough about bones to decide whether it had been caused by a bullet, a knife, or a fall off a horse. It would be hard to prove anything from what remained of him, except that the guys who had positively identified him from what the buzzards had left behind were damn fools. I put him back into shape and screwed the coffin lid down.

There was a can of putty in the suitcase, but I didn't bother doing a neat repair job. I didn't want to crowd my luck too far. I heaved the coffin back into the niche, wedged the headstone in place by jamming the camphor-soaked handkerchief into the top crack with my screwdriver, and scraped up most of the loose mortar from the floor with my hands. The mortar I dumped into the suitcase on top of the burglar kit. With the paper flowers back in the middle of the floor, the cave looked pretty neat.

I said, "You can *descanse en paz* now, friend. Good luck to you." Then I picked up my suitcase and peeked through the grille. Nobody was in sight but the bees, still zooming around the bushes.

Going over the crest of the hill, I tried to whistle. But the reaction had set in, and the muscles around my mouth twitched so bad I couldn't keep my face in shape. I twitched all over. My hands were wet, my mouth was dry, my nose burned from the camphor fumes, my stomach muscles hurt, I wanted a drink, I wanted to throw my head back and howl like a wolf just to get it out of my system. Instead, I scuffed along in the middle of the dirt road carrying my suitcase and trying to whistle "My Sweet Little Alice-Blue Gown," not getting a note out. I couldn't even wet my lips.

The car was about a hundred and fifty yards down the hill slope. Sideburns' big bay stallion was munching grass by the side of the road. A barefooted *roto* had the hood of the car up, his nose in the engine. Another pair of bare feet stuck out from under the back of the car where another *roto* was peering at the muffler. Sideburns leaned against the car, one arm lying along the top of the car behind Idaho's head, talking into her ear.

He didn't see me coming until I was practically in his hip pocket. In his position, I wouldn't have seen a herd of elephants coming down the road. Idaho was standing with her back to the car, one heel hooked up on the running board so that her knee showed, her hands behind her and her breasts stuck out like a movie star posing for a pin-up. I don't know what he was saying to her, but from his expression it was pretty personal.

Sideburns finally woke up to the fact that he had company. When he recognized me, he jerked his arm down from behind Idaho's head and put it closer to his gun. He scowled.

I put the suitcase down in the dirt, wiped my face, and jerked a thumb questioningly in the direction the car was pointed, hitching a ride from a stranger.

"The slob doesn't understand English," I said to Idaho. "How are you doing?"

"He's awful." She turned a bright smile at Sideburns. "I can't listen to much more. He's *awful!*"

"Would you say that you had been insulted?"

"If I haven't been, it hasn't been because he didn't try."

"That's fine."

Sideburns gave me an ugly look.

"What are you doing here?"

"Walking, friend. I enjoy the countryside. The lady has offered me a ride. She says that you have insulted her."

He sneered at me, as if he enjoyed sneering.

"*Véte,*" he said. "Continue walking."

His hand stopped at his hip.

I brought my own hands up chest high, making no sudden movements, and curled my fingers. He watched them, like a dope, so he didn't see me moving my feet at the same time. At the last minute he woke up, but he was really a dope. He tried to pull his gun.

I hit him on the nose first, because I had promised to hit him on the nose, and then I cracked him good on the chin. Before he could fall down, I smacked him again. He wasn't completely out when he hit the dirt, but he wasn't good for anything. He didn't argue when I took his gun and waved it at the *roto* whose eyes were bugging at me under the lifted hood.

"Put the hood down, boy," I said. "Tell your friend to get out from under the car."

He did what he was told. I watched Sideburns put his hand to his nose, take it away, and blink at the blood. He still didn't know what had happened.

I said to Idaho, "Where's the fuse?"

"In my purse. In the front seat."

I found the fuse in her purse and switched it for the dead one. By that time Sideburns was sitting up, holding his face with both hands. He wasn't interested in anything else. I threw my bag into the back seat, helped Idaho into the driver's seat, and climbed in beside her.

"That's all. Let's go."

Passing the *hacienda,* I tossed the gun out the window. We had gone another four or five kilometers before Idaho said anything.

"How—what did you find?"

"A skeleton."

"Whose?"

"Damned if I know. It wasn't Parker."

14

THEY slammed me into the can so hard that I made a billiard off three walls.

It wasn't more than two hours after I got back to Santiago, so I guess it hadn't taken Sideburns long to wake up to what was going on, have a look at the grave, and get to the nearest telephone. I had let Idaho drop me on a side street and told her to go on home after she got rid of the car, promising to see her later in the day. First I had to wash the sweat, mortar and dust off myself. Not expecting the other side to work so fast, I took my suitcase full of burglar tools back to the hotel with me and stood it in a corner. When the *carabineros* came pounding on the door, it was the first thing they saw. They had me with my pants down.

The *cárcel,* as South American *cárceles* go, wasn't bad. I was charged with *asalto, robo, transgresión, violación de sepulcro,* and *destrucción de bienes,* roughly, assault, theft, trespass, grave robbery, and destructtion of property. Señor don Rodolfo Ruano had made the charges.

Even after the iron door clanged behind me, I wasn't too much worried. They might keep me on ice for a few days, but I could blow myself out with what I knew whenever I wanted to use it. And I was a United States citizen. The *carabineros* didn't think it was safe to keep me from using a telephone, after I howled about it for a while.

First I called the embassy. The ambassador wasn't there so I talked to somebody else and told him I was in the clink.

He wanted to know what for. I said assault, theft, trespass, grave robbery and destruction of property, but that the theft charge wasn't justified. It had only been a gun, and I had returned it.

He said, My goodness, what about the other charges?

I explained that technically they might be made to stick. That was why I wanted the embassy to help me.

He almost blew out the telephone system yelling at me. Didn't I know that I was subject to Chilean law just like everyone else in the country? Didn't I realize that the embassy couldn't interfere with the orderly process of justice of another sovereign state? (Those were his words.) Did I think that my citizenship was a cloak under which I could do this and that and thus and so and the other until I hung up.

Explaining things over the phone was out. I thought of calling don Rodolfo and talking turkey to him privately, but I wasn't ready to talk turkey until I held all the high cards. Idaho could help me, but she was in the clear and I wanted to keep her in the clear. Lee was my best bet.

The *carabineros* said I could make one more call. I finally got through to Valpo and caught Lee in his office.

"Hi, there," he said. "What's new?"

"I'm in the can in Santiago."

"What?"

"I'm in the Santiago city hoosegow, charged with too many things to tell you about. I've got to talk to you. How soon can you get here?"

"I can't get there. I'm a busy man. Why don't you call the embassy? What happened? Why do you do these things?"

"I called the embassy. They want too many explanations, and I can't explain over the phone. You've got to come here and get me out. It's important."

He groaned.

"Al, I can't. You know I want to help you, but if the embassy won't interfere, what can I do? You haven't any official position. If it were a diplomatic matter . . ."

"It could be."

"What do you mean?"

The jailhouse boys were standing right beside me all this time. I didn't know how much English they understood. I said, "False statements under oath to one of Uncle's representatives. That's all I can say, but I've got solid proof. Will you come?"

Lee was a good boy. All he needed was an excuse. He said, "I'll be there in two hours. Hold your hat."

I went back to the *calabozo* and listened to the locks snick into place behind me.

They opened up again half an hour later. The turnkey said I had a lady visitor.

I thought it was Idaho. I was going to tell her to shut

up and beat it before she opened her mouth, but when I reached the room where my visitor waited, there was Terry. And I'll be damned if she wasn't wearing a silver-fox cape, this time. Imagine anyone with three fur coats.

"Ahl," she said. Her voice quavered. "Ahl."

"Hello."

Her face, white and worried, was still the best single arrangement of female features I had ever seen. I had to admit it, even though I knew where she stood. I couldn't seem to take my eyes off her mouth, with the raspberry lipstick on it. I could still taste those raspberries.

"Ahl," she said "What have you done?"

"Didn't your father tell you?" She was speaking English, so I did. There was a *carabinero* in the room with us.

"He told me that you broke into the grave. It was a terrible thing to do, Ahl. They can send you to prison for that."

"Maybe I will send somebody else to prison instead."

"For what?"

"Murder."

It didn't hit. She only looked blank.

I said, "If not murder, I'll find something else. Your uncle Robert isn't buried in that grave."

"You know that now. But what else do you know?"

I wasn't going to answer her truthfully, so I didn't answer at all. She came up close to me and put her hand on my arm.

"You found it out. But you know nothing else, and if you go to prison you will never be able to learn anything

else. Even after you get out, they will not let you remain
in the country, Ahl. And you may be years in prison. I
can persuade my father to let you go, if you will promise
to give this up, now. Will you promise?"

Her honey-colored eyes were big enough to drown me
like a fly caught in molasses. I thought of Idaho sticking
out her breasts and smiling a come-on at Sideburns on
the road to the Hacienda Quilpué, while all the time he
was making her sick to her stomach. I wondered if it
made Terry sick to her stomach to stand there with her
hand on my arm, looking up at me out of those big
pleading eyes.

I said, "Terry, I've got nothing against you. If you get
hurt in this mess, I'm sorry. I'm sorry for your father
and your mother and your brother if they get hurt, but
there's nothing I can do about it. You—all of you—have
made it impossible for me to quit. You've made me
spend too much time and too much money that wasn't
mine finding out something you could have told me at
the beginning. I've got to learn the rest of it."

"Can you do it from inside a prison?"

"Your father won't send me to prison. If you think he
is serious about trying it, remind him that I can put you
and him and Fito away for perjury. The United States
Government will be the prosecuting witness, in case he
thinks he can buy his way out of trouble."

She bit her red lips.

I said, "I won't do it if I can avoid it. I don't want to
hurt anybody unnecessarily. I'll overlook the fact that
you had Idaho Farrell fired from her job because she

helped me, and I'll . . ."

"Idaho Farrell?" The name didn't mean a thing to her.

"The girl at the bank. The one whom you met at my hotel."

"I had her fired?"

"You told your father that you had seen her with me, then, and he had her fired. You also told him that I was going to Antofagasta. He followed me there, and either shot at me himself or had me shot at. I'll overlook that, too. But . . ."

I stopped. There was too much horror in her face to have been faked.

"They—they tried to *kill* you?"

"I won't say that. But somebody took a shot at me."

"It wasn't my father! Believe me, Ahl!" She was holding my arm with both hands. "He wouldn't try to harm you. If I hadn't been sure of that, I would never have told him that you were going. Never!"

She shook me, seeing my expression.

"He followed me to Antofagasta."

"No."

"Yes."

"No!"

"I saw his name on the flight list of the plane."

"You couldn't have! He hasn't left the house since we went to the consulate."

"Rodolfo Ruano was on the plane that left before mine. If you want to see for yourself . . ."

"Fito! He did it. I'll—I'll . . ."

She was so mad she couldn't speak. Her eyes blazed. As for me, I let my chin drop down on my chest like a suitcase lid.

Because there was the key to the big puzzle, staring me right in the eye, and I hadn't seen it. I won't say I saw it all at once, even then, but I saw where the key went into the lock, and later I figured out how to twist it. All I could think of at that moment was: Fito means Rodolfito means Little Rodolfo. Al means Alvin means the original Peruvian Pinhead. Oh, you great big wonderful knot-headed dumb chowderbrain!

What I said was, "That's right. Fito's name is Rodolfo, too, isn't it?"

"He followed you! My father didn't know it, Ahl! I swear he didn't. I didn't know it either! I wouldn't have let him! I wouldn't let anybody—not even my father—h-hurt you . . ."

I simply wasn't paying any attention to what she said. My head was buzzing like a clock getting ready to strike fourteen. I just stared at her.

The tears welled up in her eyes and overflowed. She didn't sob or sniffle or screw up her mouth. She just cried, holding her face together and her chin up while the tears streaked her cheeks and I stood there with a blank expression and watched her.

It only lasted a moment. She turned away. The *carabinero* opened the door for her. Then he took me back to my cell.

By the time Lee got there, I was as jumpy as a flea. I had to get out of hock and get busy clearing up the tag ends. Lee wanted to know what it was all about, of course—particularly the perjury angle. I stalled him. As long as he wasn't officially on notice about it, he wouldn't have to do anything. I didn't want anything done until I was ready for it. I had a tough time convincing him that he ought to bail me out just on my say-so, but after I promised to tell him the whole story when I knew it and gave him my word that I wouldn't skip the country and leave him holding the sack, he went to bat for me.

I was on the street at five o'clock. The first plane for Antofagasta took off at five forty-five. I made it by the skin of my teeth.

It got in about nine-thirty. I took a taxi from the airport to the Club Unión and found Willie Humphreys exactly where I had left him, a gin rickey in his hand, his nose glowing like a red-hot poker, the double wingback freezeout lined up against him at the far side of the *cantina*.

I said, "Remember me, Willie?"

"Sure. Glad to see you again, son. Siddown."

He didn't remember me from a plate of spaghetti.

I said, "My name is Al Colby. I was here talking to you about Roberto Ruano a couple of days ago."

"Always glad to meet a friend of Roberto Ruano. Fine lad. I remember once . . ."

I pulled up a chair and sat down facing him while he wound up. As soon as he stopped talking long enough to suck at the rickey, I cut in.

"Look, Willie. You knew Roberto Ruano in the old days, when you were both working in the nitrate fields.

He went away twenty years ago, and you never saw him again. Is that right?"

"That's right. Always wondered what happened to him. We used to play billiards . . ."

"He was a young man then, under thirty-five. Is that right?"

"Yep. He would have been about that, all right. I . . ."

"I asked you the other night if you knew Rodolfo Ruano. I told you he was Roberto's brother, and you said you had played billiards with him, too. You said . . ."

"Sure did. He . . ."

"Wait a minute. I want you to think hard. It's been more than twenty years since you saw Roberto, remember. How long ago did you play billiards with Rodolfo here in the club?"

He buried his nose in the rickey glass and thought hard, trying to sort out the jumble that was his memory. Because I was pretty sure of myself, I said, "Five or six years ago?"

"About that, I guess. Seems to me it wasn't long back."

"About how old was he then?"

"Must have been around Roberto's age, I guess. Just a lad. We . . ."

"Hold it. Five or six years ago, Rodolfo was about the same age as Roberto was when you last knew him, twenty years back. Rodolfo really was twenty or twenty-five years younger than Roberto. Isn't that right?"

He worked hard on that one. The cogs kept slipping on him, but he finally guessed I was right. It seemed strange to him that two brothers should be born that far apart. It just went to show that a man was as good as his . . .

"I told you that they were brothers," I said. "I was wrong. Rodolfo is Roberto's son. They call him Fito."

His face lit up.

"Why, sure. Sure he is. Hell, I remember when he was born. I went to his christening, right here in Antofagasta."

It was as easy as that.

I bought Willie a gin rickey and had the boy at the desk call me a taxi. There was a victoria stand near the club, but a victoria was too slow. Fito and his old man might or might not know where I was, and they might or might not try to have me knocked off. I wasn't sure. I sat low in the taxi until we reached the Hotel Maury, and I didn't waste any time getting under cover.

The first plane south that had room for me left at six in the morning. It put me down in Santiago around ten. I telephoned Lee from the airport, as I had promised to do as soon as I got back to town, and learned that don Rodolfo had been kicking up because I had been released in Lee's custody. Don Rodolfo wanted me back in the tank where I belonged. He had complained to the embassy, and the embassy was riding Lee's tail about it.

I said, "They won't be riding you for long. I'm going to see don Rodolfo right now. When I get through talking to him, he'll be a good boy."

"I hope you're right. I've gone out on a limb for you, Al. If anything goes wrong . . ."

"Nothing will go wrong. I'll be seeing you."

I hung up and went straight from the airport to the house on Avenida O'Higgins.

Terry and Fito were in the *patio* when I got there. They were talking about me, as I knew from their angry expressions and the way they shut up when the maid brought me into the *patio*. They both looked mad and worried at the same time.

Fito stood up, his face ugly.

"You are not welcome in this house, Mr. Colby. You should know that."

"I came to see your father. If he will not see me here, I will meet him at his convenience."

"He will not see you."

"Will you ask him?"

"No."

Terry said, "That will not help, Fito."

She rang the bell.

She did not look at me while we waited for the maid to come back. But I looked at her. I wanted her to meet my eyes. I wanted her to see that I had forgotten what she tried to sell me in jail, that she had left nothing with me that might shame her. A girl was justified in using any weapon to protect someone she loved. I wanted her to know that I realized that. I wasn't even sore at Fito because of the bullet. I wasn't sore at anybody, any more. I wished they would both understand I was only doing a job.

She never looked at me.

The maid showed up. Terry told her to ask don Rodolfo

to come to the *patio*. We waited.

Don Rodolfo bowed silently when he saw me. His icy expression didn't change.

I said, "I apologize for violating your hospitality, don Rodolfo. There are some things we must discuss. If you would prefer to meet me at another place . . ."

"I have said that my house is yours, *señor*. What have you to discuss with me?"

"It would be better that we talk alone."

He didn't budge. I said, "You once offered me the courtesies of your billiard room. I should like to enjoy them again."

That puzzled him. He didn't know how to refuse me. Finally he bowed again and turned away. I followed him.

We were at the archway when Terry said, "Father."

He turned. So did I.

"No tengas pena."

Terry smiled at him, her chin up. Fito stood at her side, jaw set, fists clenched, his eyes dark.

Do not have grief. It bucked the old boy, if he needed bucking. He knew where he stood with his kids, whatever happened. He inclined his head and motioned me on.

We went down to the billiard room.

The portrait of doña María hung on the wall with his others. It was a wonderful job. He had caught the look in her face that I tried to describe.

I said, "An excellent painting, don Rodolfo. Doña María is well?"

"She has had a touch of *fiebre*. Nothing serious."

He thought I was playing with him. I wasn't. I wanted to get it over with as much as he did, but I didn't know how to start. Because I didn't say anything, he gestured at the billiard table. The balls were already set up.

"Will you play as we talk?"

"With pleasure."

We chalked up the cues. He wanted me to take the break, because the break is an easy billiard. I wanted him to take it, I won the argument.

He squared off.

As he stroked the cue ball, I said, in English, "It's my turn to win, Parker."

15

HE MISSED the shot a mile. He didn't even hit his object ball. Still he tried to pretend that he hadn't understood me, looking up with his eyebrows raised as if to question me politely for forgetting that he didn't speak English.

I said, "It's no use. I've got you cold."

"*¿Perdone?*"

"It was a good scheme. But I should have known that anybody smart enough to carry two names with a single passport wouldn't find it hard to think up another twist."

"If you will speak Spanish, please. I am confused . . ."

"I'm not. Not any more. All you had to do was die, and everything went to your son, Rodolfo. You became Rodolfo as well—two of you in the same house, the same name, the same loyalties, the same person in two bodies —don Rodolfo Ruano, heir to the family properties whether you called him brother or son, still keeping everything that Roberto had before he died except the identity that was no longer safe for you to keep. You fooled me for a long time."

He shook his head, puzzled.

"I am sorry. I have little English. I do not understand you."

"Oh, give it up! It won't take me an hour to prove that Roberto Ruano Parker never had a brother. It won't take me five minutes to put you down on the floor and look at your teeth, if you want it that way. I tell you, it's all over!"

We were facing each other. He had the billiard cue in his hand, holding it short, just at the right balance to clip me alongside the ear with the loaded butt end. I saw the thought come to him. Then he sighed, walked over to the rack, and put the cue away carefully.

"Yes," he said, in English. "It's all over. What now?"

"Talk."

"About what?"

"You. Why did you run out?"

"Does it make a difference?"

"I want to know all the answers. I'm not a cop, and I've got nothing against you. I don't want to kick over your applecart any more than I have to."

"Thank you. Where do you want me to begin?"

"At the beginning."

There were a couple of chairs against the wall. He pulled them out. We sat down. He thought for a while, staring blankly at the floor.

"Excuse me if I speak Spanish," he said at last. "I have avoided speaking English or listening to it for so long that it no longer comes easily to me."

"One language is as good as another."

"Truly." He sighed. "*Pues,* my wife—doña María—and I were married nearly thirty years ago. We had the two children you know. I had made much money from the nitrate properties my father left me, and our marriage was happy, but I was young and accustomed to a more active life than marriage and a family offered me in Antofagasta, where we lived. Antofagasta is not an exciting place. I grew discontented as the years passed. Doña María was happy with her house and children. I wanted to know the world.

"I went to the States on what I told my wife was a business trip. Because it was not a business trip, and because I meant to be free of all restraint, I called myself Robert R. Parker, using my mother's name, and said nothing about my *chileno* background. I spoke English, then, as naturally as the Americans from whom I had learned it in the nitrate fields, and passed easily for an American.

"In California, I met the woman I married there. I was thirty-five. She was much younger, eighteen or nineteen, and beautiful. I fell in love with her. I wanted her more than I had ever wanted anything. She was— then, at least—chaste, and I could not have her without marriage. I think now that I could not have had her, even with marriage, had she not realized that I was wealthy. I had taken money with me, and I was free with it. That was all she knew of me, but it was enough. I was young and a fool. With no remorse, no thought for my true wife and children, I abandoned them and married Helen."

I said, "You need not punish yourself unnecessarily."

"I am not punishing myself. I am simply telling you the truth."

He paused for a moment before he went on.

"I invested my money in real estate and made more, much more, so I could give her everything she wanted—except youth. She was a child when we married. When I was fifty, she was thirty-three, at the peak of her beauty. She was—she was . . ."

He moved his hands helplessly.

"It is hard for me to describe her. Did you ever see her?"

"No."

"Then you can not understand how I felt. I knew that she was vain, and ill-mannered and cruel, a bad woman at heart, yet I would have done anything for her. She wanted parties, excitement, gaiety. I could give her those, but her friends were all of her own age. I was 'the old man' to them—Helen's 'old man.' She joked about it, to my face. It hurt, but I bore with it. I might be her 'old man' but I loved her, and she was still my wife—or so I thought, until I discovered that she had been unfaithful to me. Not once but many times, and with friends I had accepted in my home."

The mask slipped when he said that. I saw his mouth twist. But he went on talking in the same level voice.

"I asked her to deny what I had heard. She laughed and called me an old fool to think that I could hold her.

"I meant to kill her, at first. But fifteen years in California had taught me to think like a *norteamericano,* with the head instead of the heart. Her death would serve no purpose. My honor was already such a shabby thing that another stain more or less meant little. I thought of taking my own life, but that was the short escape of a coward. If I owed Helen nothing, there was still a debt to be paid to my true wife and children. Fifteen years too late, I realized this.

"It was not an easy thing to do, but I made up my mind to come back. Even if I could not recover what I had thrown away, I still might be able to repay some part of what I owed. I had careful inquiries made. I learned that doña María, after taking those steps which were necessary to satisfy herself that Roberto Ruano did not die in the States, had guessed that I was deserting her. She was too proud to investigate further, or to try to bring me back against my will. She took the children to La Paz, in Bolivia, where her parents lived, so she need not explain to Antofagasta why her husband had left her. But Fito, when he became a man, had to return to attend to matters concerning the family proerties. I was too much of a coward to beg doña María to take me back. I wrote Fito, asking him if there could be forgiveness in his heart and his sister's and his mother's for an old man who did not deserve forgiveness. He wrote back immediately. He said—he said . . ."

The Spanish grandee had to swallow before he could go on. His eyes glowed.

I said, "You need not tell me what he wrote. I know how your children feel toward their father."

I took Fito's photograph out of my pocket and handed it to him.

"This is yours. It was found in the car you sold in Mexico."

"Thank you. It was a great loss to me."

He studied the picture for a moment before he closed his hand around it.

"What more do you want to know? I obtained a United States passport . . ."

"I know that part of it. What did you tell doña María?"

"I lied to her, in a sense, although it does not weigh on my conscience. I told her only that I had committed a crime, and that all the steps I took to conceal my identity were necessary for my protection. She loves me enough to ask no more questions than I wish to answer. It would break her heart to know that I am a—bigamist."

"Your children know?"

"Yes. I had to tell them everything, because I wanted their help in the conspiracy to protect their mother from learning the truth. They have forgiven me."

"Few men are fortunate enough to have a family such as yours."

"I know. I do not deserve them. It makes my happiness complete to realize that."

His face was like a rock as he sat there spilling his guts to the stranger who was tearing down all that he had built up so carefully. His hands rested in his lap, holding Fito's photograph. He waited for me to deal the cards he would have to play out.

I said, "Why did you not stay in Bolivia with your family, instead of returning to Chile? It would have been harder to trace you there."

"I know. But all of our money comes from Chile, which restricts exportation of funds. In Chile I am a wealthy man, in Bolivia I would have been a pauper living on the charity of doña María's family and what little money Fito could smuggle out to us from Antofagasta. I did not know then that I had made a mistake in failing to sign over the California properties to Helen, but I knew her nature. I would never be wholly safe in Chile as Roberto Ruano Parker. With Fito's help I bought the *fundo* near Melipilla and lived there long enough to arrange things so that all my property would go to him at my death. Then—I died. Rodolfo Ruano—both Rodolfo Ruanos—came to live here, and María Teresa and her mother came down to join us from La Paz. Since neither doña María nor I entertain visitors or find it necessary to appear in public, there is very little chance that anyone we knew twenty years ago in Antofagasta will ever recognize us. We have been very happy here"

"Until I came."

"Until you came."

I thought about what he had told me. He watched my face.

I said, "Who lies in your grave on the Hacienda Quilpué?"

"A cattle thief."

"How did he die?"

"Víctor Chavarría—the man whose nose you broke yesterday—caught him stealing stock and shot him. We took his body to a remote section of the *fundo,* dressed it in my clothes, killed my horse beside it, and left both for the buzzards. Meanwhile I stayed away from the *ha-*

cienda and grew the beard you see. Later, when Víctor brought the body in and identified it as my own, I also identified it for the benefit of the local *alcalde*. He was a stupid man, not hard to deceive."

"You made Chavarría your *administrador* to pay him for the murder?"

"Murder?" He seemed surprised. "It is not murder to shoot a cattle thief."

"Has the law decided that?"

He still seemed surprised—a little too much so. I said, "I know you have convinced your family that the killing was justifiable. But even if it happened as you say it did—and it seems strange to me that a body should turn up just when you needed it—I think the law would call it murder. I think what probably happened was that you had Chavarría go out and make you a body when you needed one. I know he would have enjoyed the job."

The old man didn't argue. He waited for me to go on.

I said, "It's nothing to me how or why you killed him, or what other crimes you have committed, but so far you are open to charges for bigamy, perjury, murder, and a few other things. I might not be able to do anything to Fito for taking a shot at me, but I can get him for perjury. Your daughter, too."

He said calmly, "If my crimes are nothing to you, why do you remind me of them?"

"I don't want any difficulty when I take you back to California."

He smiled, shaking his head.

"I am not going back to California, Señor Colby. Never."

"It's the easiest way. I'm doing you a favor. You have to sign papers releasing the title of the California properties to your wife. In California you can do it without publicity. Down here, it means that you would have to appear before a United States consul and identify yourself as Robert R. Parker. That would automatically perjure you for swearing that Parker, Roberto Ruano, and the body in the grave are all the same, besides opening up the question of the cattle thief's death. And the papers you would have to sign would show that you had another wife living in the States. The only possible thing for you to do is come back with me."

He shook his head again, still smiling.

"No."

I was beginning to get mad. I said, "All right. Then I'll have the papers sent down here, and you can worry about what's going to happen to you when you sign them."

"I am not going to sign any papers. Neither here nor in California."

I couldn't believe it. It was impossible. There he was, licked, cornered, without a leg to stand on or a place to turn, telling me what he would do and what he would not do, as calmly as if he were in my place and I in his.

"All of what you say is very true," he said. "I dare not sign the papers here, and I will not go back to California. That part of my life is dead. Even if I were not sure that Helen would have me jailed for the bigamy—and I know her too well to expect anything else—I would not return. I will never go back."

I exploded.

"Man, you're crazy! You have nothing to say about it! You're beaten! She'll know about the bigamy as soon as I turn in my report. And if you refuse to sign the papers she wants, she'll have a good reason to persecute you. You can't fight her!"

"There is one way I can fight her."

I didn't get it right away. He smiled at me until I did.

I said, "You talk like a child."

"Do you think I am childish because I realize that a dead man is beyond injury?"

"I think you are foolish to talk of death when it is not necessary to die. You have too much to live for."

"I have much to live for, yes. I think I realize it more because I lived without it for so long. I will not live without it again. So long as I can keep what I have, I want to go on living. When I lose what I have, then I have had enough of life. What you propose for me would cost me my wife's faith and happiness, which I value above everything."

I got up and walked around the billiard table. If he had been any other man, I would have laughed in his face for trying to bluff me. I couldn't laugh at him. He meant every word of it.

"You have said that if I were dead there would be no need to sign any papers," he went on. "You have affidavits that say I am dead. I am sure that with those you can satisfy your courts, if you choose to. If you choose to report that the affidavits are false and that I am alive, I will prove you wrong when it becomes necessary. It is very simple."

There was a long, long time when neither of us said anything more. My own voice sounded strange when I spoke.

"You expect me to lie to the people who hired me, to keep you from taking your own life?"

"I expect nothing. And I did not say that I would take my own life. That would be a greater sin, in my wife's eyes, than anything else I might have done. I will not distress her further. I said only that I would prove you wrong if you report that I am alive."

"I must report the truth. Beyond that . . ."

"Then there is nothing more we need discuss." He stood up, motioning me courteously forward. "Shall we go upstairs?"

Doña María, Terry and Fito were all waiting for us in the *patio*. They looked like three people expecting the lights to dim when the current went on in the hot seat. Don Rodolfo—I still thought of him by that name—said something about doña María's *fiebre* and brought her a *mantilla* that hung over the back of a chair. His family watched me with scared eyes while he put the *mantilla* around his wife's shoulders.

"Señor Colby is leaving Chile soon," he said easily. "We have reached an understanding about his visit to the *fundo*. Fito, you will see that the charges against him are withdrawn."

Fito didn't say anything, just stared at me. The old

man said, "Immediately."

Fito left the *patio* without a word.

His movement broke up the death watch. Terry moved toward her mother. I muttered something about being in a hurry, thanked doña María for her hospitality, and shook her hand. Terry held out her hand automatically, so I shook that, too. Then I'll be damned if don Rodolfo didn't hold out his hand and wish me *buen viaje* as if he meant it. I stumbled up the steps that led out of the *patio*. My head was going round and round. I couldn't think straight.

Terry's heels came clicking along behind me as I went through the hall. I couldn't get the front door open before she caught me.

"Ahl," she said, putting her back against the door. "What happened? What are you going to do?"

"Leave me alone."

"What are you going to do about my father?"

"Leave me alone. Go away."

"Please listen to me, Ahl. He is an old man. My mother . . ."

"Get away from that door!"

I pulled her clear of the door so I could get it open.

At least that's what I meant to do. It wasn't my idea to collect a last bribe before I sold her father down the river. But when I put my hand on her, she came into my arms, her own arms tight around my neck, her mouth on mine, clinging to me so strongly that I had to use both hands to break her grip. It was her last chance to buy me off, and she did her best. I was panting like a blown horse when I finally pushed her off, yanked the door open, and ran.

16

IDAHO and I got drunk that night. Strictly speaking, I got drunk while she hung around and kept an eye on me. I think she stuck to lemonade most of the evening, but the weather got too hazy for me to recollect the details. I remember that when I picked her up at her *pensión* she wanted to know what had happened and what I was going to do about old man Ruano. After I told her that I didn't feel like talking about it, she stopped asking questions. I did a lot of drinking and forgot to eat. The last I remember, I was sitting on a bed trying to get my shoes off and hang on to a bottle at the same time. I forget whether I gave up the shoes or the bottle first.

It was my own bed, when I woke up in it next morning. Idaho was lying beside me, fast asleep, one bare arm behind her head. She looked about sixteen.

My heart went right down to where my shoes would have been if somebody hadn't taken them off for me. I must have made some kind of a noise, because she woke up.

She was startled, at first. Then she smiled. I smiled, feeling my face crack like a slab of dried mud.

"How do you feel?" she said.

"Terrible."

I couldn't think of anything else to say, so I got a cigarette off the table by the side of the bed. It tasted like horsehair, but I smoked it down to the last half inch and burned my fingers putting it out.

"Idaho."

"Yes?"

"I'm sorry about this. I don't know how it happened."

"Sorry about what?"

"Us. Here. I know I was drunk, but I didn't realize— I didn't think . . ."

"I wasn't drunk, if that's what you mean. I knew what I was doing."

"Oh."

We lay there, side by side, a million miles apart. I didn't know how to break it up. She turned to me suddenly, putting her cheek against mine.

"Don't feel sorry for anything on my account, Al," she whispered. "Please."

I held her for a minute. Then she pulled away.

"Now I'm going to get dressed," she said cheerfully. "I don't suppose you are gentleman enough to look the other way when I get out of bed, are you?"

"No."

I wasn't, either. Even feeling as awful as I did, it was a treat just to watch her move while she gathered up her clothes and disappeared into the bathroom. I never saw a woman who was more worth gawping at.

While she was in the bathroom, the phone rang. I didn't answer it. It stopped ringing after a while. A few minutes later it rang again. I lay there, not thinking, just feeling my head throb, until somebody knocked at the door. I didn't move. Pretty soon a letter and a slip of paper came sliding under the door. The boy outside went away.

I got up.

The slip of paper was a telephone message. Señorita Ruano had called and was very anxious to get in touch with Señor Colby about a matter of extreme urgency. I tore it up.

The letter was from Adams, marked Special Delivery, Urgent, Please Forward. Inside was a note that didn't say anything in particular except time is of the essence, and a passport photograph of Robert R. Parker, don Rodolfo minus the beard and with less white in his hair. But just as an indication of how thoroughly he had had me fooled, I knew that if I hadn't tumbled to him before the photograph arrived I would have thought he and his brother had a strong family resemblance. It goes to show that a sucker is always willing to cooperate when somebody else wants to sucker him.

I wasn't as pretty to look at in the raw as Idaho was, so I put on a robe before she came out of the bathroom. She looked slick, her hair combed and her makeup where it belonged. I soaked myself in the tub for half an hour, shaved, brushed my teeth, ate a couple of aspirins, and felt better.

Idaho was still there when I came out of the bathroom. I didn't want to put up with any wise looks from the kid who ran the elevator, so I let Idaho go downstairs first and followed her five minutes later. Nobody told me to kindly pack my bags and move.

While we were eating breakfast, I asked her what her plans were.

"I haven't any. I'm still working for you. Remember?"

"The job is finished here. I'm going back to Mexico."

"Oh." She fiddled with a spoon. "Well, I still owe you twenty-eight days on the first month's salary."

"You don't think you can get another job here?"

"Not in Chile. My work *permiso* was canceled when the bank fired me."

"Want to go back to the States?"

"I guess I'll have to."

"You could stop over in Mexico until the twenty-eight days are worked out, if you like."

"What would I be doing?"

"Same things."

"All right."

After breakfast I sent her back to her *pensión* to start packing, then went on to the Panagra office to see about plane tickets. I still had the reservation I had bought for a decoy before going to Antofagasta the second time, but the plane left early that same afternoon. I wouldn't be able to make it even if they could give me another ticket for Idaho, which they couldn't. But they had a couple of cancellations on the northbound flight the next morning.

That left me the rest of the day to pick up Idaho's passport and get it and my own decorated with the red tape they wind around you whenever you are trying to leave any South American country. I broke all records. By nightfall, when I crawled back to the hotel, I was so dog-tired from hammering at dumb officials that I couldn't see straight, but I had the *permisos, certificados* and visas I needed to get us both out of Chile the next day. That and a good soft bed was all I wanted to think about. My conscience hurt because I was sneaking out without telling Lee the whole story, but he had no responsibility for me now. And I didn't feel like discussing the job with anybody.

The desk clerk gave me half a dozen telephone messages with my key. They were all from Terry. I crumpled them up as I walked away from the desk, looking for a wastebasket.

The nearest one was under a writing table where a big chair faced the elevators. Somebody was sitting in the big chair. I didn't see who it was until I reached the wastebasket.

It was Terry. She looked terrible. There were lines in her face I hadn't noticed before.

She said, "I have to talk to you, Ahl."

"Did your father tell you what we talked about yesterday?"

"Yes."

"Then there isn't anything more to say. I'm sorry. I've been beating my brains out trying to think of the right thing to do, but I've got to do it myself. Arguing with you will just make it harder for both of us."

"I didn't come to argue. I came to warn you."

"Warn me?"

"Against Fito."

"What's he up to?"

"Nothing that I am sure of. But he hasn't been home all day and I know him so well. I'm afraid of what he might do."

"What do you expect him to do—shoot at me again?"

"He could. He said he meant it only as a warning the first time. It would not be a warning if he did it again. He would kill you."

"What good does he think that would do?"

She made a hopeless, angry gesture.

"He does not think sensibly, like a man. He is still a small boy who loves his father and mother and would do anything to prevent shame from coming to them. If my father goes back to California and is jailed for big-amy, it will break my mother's heart. Fito would kill you to prevent that."

"Did your father say anything about going back to California?"

She looked up from the ring she was twisting around her finger.

"What else can he do? It would be much worse if he signed the papers here."

For a minute I almost felt happy. If don Rodolfo had been bluffing me, and really meant to go back to California without a struggle, I was in the clear. There might be a broken heart on my conscience, but a broken heart isn't blood.

The feeling didn't last. I remembered his face when he told me how he would fight Dear Helen. He hadn't been bluffing with me. The bluff had been saved for his kids.

I said, "All right, Terry. I'll look out for Fito. Thanks for coming to tell me."

"I do not want my brother to be a murderer."

"You don't think much of me, do you?"

She didn't answer.

I said, "You think I'm scum because I took your kisses without giving you what you expected to get for them. All right. It was a scummy thing to do. But I didn't desert a wife and children, or commit bigamy, or perjure myself, or have a man killed to fill an empty grave. Your father did those things. It's not my fault that he has to pay for them. I've got no more to do with it than the postman who brings him bad news in a letter. If I could help him, make it easier for him in any way, I'd do it. I don't enjoy hurting people. I have a job to do. Can't you get that through your head?"

I was talking too loud before I finished. People turned to stare at us. Terry didn't say anything. She stood up and walked away. Her face was as white as a bone.

I didn't sleep very well that night. In the morning I made five or six attempts to draft a cable to Adams. It wouldn't come out right. I couldn't call it back once it was on its way, and I kept seeing the old man's smile. I finally gave it up, kidding myself with the idea that I would have the answer by the time I reached Mexico.

Fito was still on my mind. He was just crazy enough to take a shot at me right there in the hotel, without a thought for what would happen to him afterward. I went down to the desk about 6 A.M.—I used the stairs, taking a good look around the lobby before I stepped into the open—and paid my bill. My bags were all packed. The clerk said he'd have them delivered to the airport not later than nine o'clock, *sin falta*. From the hotel I went to Idaho's *pensión* and stayed there until it was time to go to the airport.

Fito had to be waiting for me there, if he really meant business. We were supposed to show up for baggage inspection the usual hour ahead of time, but I cut it fine. It was fifteen minutes before plane time when our taxi made the turn into the airport.

I said to Idaho, "I'm expecting a little trouble in the next couple of minutes. I think I'll be able to talk myself out of it, but you never can tell. Here are the tickets and all the money I have. My bags came on ahead. Check them through customs for me, if you can. Whatever happens, get on the plane. Your ticket is good to Mexico City. The money will get you from there to New York and leave you some over."

She turned pale. Before she could speak, I said, "It isn't as bad as it sounds. I'm just taking precautions. Give me a kiss, and don't wait for me when the taxi stops."

She turned her face up. I kissed her. The taxi-driver put on his brakes, pulling around in a sharp circle that left us parked in front of the entrance to the waiting room.

Idaho gave me no trouble. She left the taxi and went up the steps and through the door without looking back.

I paid the driver, told him to hurry the lady's bags along, and followed Idaho.

Fito was waiting for me just inside the door. He had his hand in his coat pocket. I turned cold all over, for a second, expecting to feel the slug in my ribs.

"Colby!"

I was looking straight ahead. I turned my head, surprised to see him.

"Hello, Fito. What are you doing here?"

"I want to talk with you."

Even if I hadn't known that there was a gun in his pocket, I could have guessed it from his expression. He looked about twenty years older than he had the first time I saw him. Little bunches of muscle stood out over the corners of his mouth.

I said, "Well, come along," as if it didn't matter, and kept moving. He had to follow or shoot me in the back. He didn't shoot.

I knew I could take him, then. A man who has a gun but isn't ready and willing to use it at any minute is worse off than a man without a gun, because he has to be trying to make up his mind to pull the trigger while the guy without the gun, not having to worry about anything but his reflexes, simply hauls off and slaps the first guy silly. All I needed for Fito was a good place to lay him down.

There was a door across the way marked CABAL-LEROS. A man came out of it just as I got there. Fito was a step behind me when I went through the door.

I don't know just how I would have worked it had

there been anyone in the washroom, but it was empty, unless somebody was using one of the toilet booths. I wasn't worried about anyone who couldn't see us. As I heard the whoosh from the compressed-air gadget that let the door close without slamming, I turned around to Fito with a big smile.

"Say, I've got good news for you, Fito."

There wasn't a man living who, in his position, could have pulled the trigger on me then without first listening to what I had to say. I took his elbow in my left hand, pulled him around as if I were going to whisper something cozy in his ear—it moved the muzzle of the gun out of line with my belly, just in case—and hit him on the chin as he turned into the punch.

He had a glass jaw. He went out like a candle in a high wind. I caught him before he fell, dragged him over to one of the booths, hooked the door open with my foot, sat him on the toilet, and took his gun. Then I cracked him over the ear with the gun-butt to keep him quiet until the plane took off.

The door of the booth had one of those locks that shows OCUPADO on a disc outside when the booth is in use. I locked the door behind me by turning the disc to OCUPADO with my finger. When I left the washroom, the loudspeaker was bellowing for Meester Colby, Meester Colby, your plane leaves in five meenutes, Meester Colby. Idaho waited by the departure gate, looking like a ghost.

Her color came back when she saw me. I waved to her as I hurried over to the ticket desk, where I got bawled

out for holding things up. The plane took off four minutes late, all on account of me.

17

I DIDN'T wire Adams when we got back to Mexico City. I knew he would be eating his fingernails off over the two hundred and fifty thousand dollar deal on the fire, but I couldn't get what I had to say into a telegram. After I had tried it about twenty times, I decided that it would be easier to write a letter.

Idaho knew shorthand. We sat down together and I dictated the letter to her.

The first part wasn't hard. I summarized what I had done since the first report, giving Adams the details about places and dates and names. It was a good report of a good job until I got to my last conversation with the old man.

There it stuck. I still couldn't put it into words. I knew, as well as I knew anything, that Parker would die before he would let Dear Helen or anybody else break up his home. But all I could quote him as saying was that he had promised not to commit suicide. It was silly on the face of it. And I couldn't end the letter by telling Adams, Here is your man, I got him for you according to orders, but you have to let him go and forget the two hundred and fifty thousand dollars because I say so. I couldn't end it at all.

I finally told Idaho to tear up her notes. The letter had gone far enough so that she knew pretty well what was bothering me, but she didn't offer any damn fool helpful suggestions. She said, "You're awfully jittery, Al. Why don't you take a vacation?"

"I can't take a vacation until I finish the report."

"You aren't making any progress with it. Maybe if you forgot about it for a few days—just relaxed and put it out of your mind—you'd be able to do it."

It was a better idea than anything I had thought of. I said, "Where would you like to go?"

"Anywhere."

"The beach?"

"If you like."

We flew down to Acapulco and rented a *cabaña* on the cliffs. The weather was wonderful. We didn't do much, just slept late, watched the *muchachos* risk their necks diving off the rocks, and lay around on the sand. A bunch of people were there from California, the Hollywood crowd, soaking up sun between pictures. Some of the girls were pretty nice to look at, but none of them had anything on Idaho in a bathing suit. Even the movie boys, who put in their eight hours a day looking at girls, turned their heads when she went by. Then they looked at me, wondering, How come? If it hadn't been for that report weighing on my mind every minute, I would have felt like a king.

The third night we were there, I squared away at it again. I waited until Idaho was asleep before I went to work. Everything was quiet, except for the boom of surf on the rocks. I felt fresh, relaxed, full of the old zing. I sharpened up a couple of pencils and sat down with a schoolboy's tablet of ruled paper.

"No more *tontería*," I said. "Get it over with. It's only a job."

"Right," I said.

That was about midnight. At 4 A.M. I broke both pencils in half, threw the pieces out the window, threw the tablet after them, and went in to wake Idaho. I was strung so tight that it made me mad to think of her sleeping while I was sweating my brains out. I shook her.

"Get up. We're going to Los Angeles."

It took a minute for her mind to start working. She said, "When?"

"On the first plane."

"Does it leave in the middle of the night?"

"Are you complaining about something?"

"I just wonder if there is some good reason why you have to come and shout at me in the middle of the night. Or is it part of my job to jump out of bed whenever you snap your fingers?"

"Excuse me for disturbing you. Excuse me all to hell and back again."

We left it there.

She got up in plenty of time to catch the plane with me. It was an excursion flight that flew non-stop to Los Angeles, and it put us down there in time to spend three hours looking for a hotel that didn't bulge with conventions. We finally found a noisy room in a place on Main Street, too late for me to see Adams that day.

Idaho was still chilly the next morning. I said, "I've got business to attend to. Do you know anybody in Los Angeles?"

"No."

"Can you entertain yourself until I get back?"

"I've done it before."

"I'll see you this afternoon, then."

"All right."

I walked over to Adams' office on Spring Street. It was like climbing the thirteen steps to the last jump-off.

Adams was a middle-aged stocky fellow who wore glasses and hadn't kept his hair. He was surprised to see me, naturally. When I told him that I had found Parker more than a week before, he didn't blow up and ask me why I hadn't cabled him. He listened. He was a good listener.

It was a lot easier to talk about than to put in a report. I told him what there was to tell, and gave him everything I had that bore on the case, including the affidavits. When I finished talking, he went right to the point.

"You don't think he was bluffing?"

"I know he wasn't bluffing. He has his home, his family, and the life he wants. If he can't keep it, he doesn't want anything."

Adams fiddled with a paper cutter.

I said, "I know he won't sign any papers in Chile as Robert Parker. It would open up too many charges against him. But if you could talk his wife—Helen—into promising to leave him alone if he came back here . . ."

Adams shook his head.

"She wouldn't promise anything. And if she did, she'd double-cross him. She's a hellion, Al—vindictive as a snake. She doesn't give a damn for Parker, but she'd jump at the chance to make trouble for him just because he left her instead of waiting for her to leave him. He'd know that, whatever promises were made."

"Wouldn't a prosecution for bigamy throw out her claim to the properties?"

"No. She has a common-law interest even if they weren't properly married."

"How about not letting her know he was here until he'd signed the papers and gone home?"

"I can't do that. I'm her lawyer. If she wants to prosecute, as she's legally entitled to do, I can't put myself in the position of having helped him escape prosecution. It would be a breach of ethics."

"What have ethics got to do with saving a man's life?"

He shrugged.

"We all have to make a living, Al."

I was sweating. It seemed a lot hotter to me there in Los Angeles than it had ever been in Mexico.

I said, "There's one other thing to do, then. You have three affidavits saying Robert Parker is dead and buried under the name of Roberto Ruano. With those . . ."

"No."

I wiped my face with the back of my hand.

"I can't do it," he said. "Even forgetting ethics, I can't put a client into a mess on fake evidence. There are too many things that could go wrong. If he ever turned up again—if anyone ever learned that he was still alive—the whole title to the property would collapse."

"Your client would have her money."

"Maybe. She would also have a two hundred-and-fifty-thousand-dollar lawsuit on her hands."

I snarled at him.

"It would fix you up just fine if he killed himself, wouldn't it?"

"I'd rather he was dead, yes. I told you in the beginning that it would simplify things. I don't want to cause his death any more than you do."

"Well, it's your baby now. I'm finished. I'll mail in my account when I get back to Mexico. Don't send me any more of your dirty business."

I took my hat off his desk and started for the door.

He said, "Why get sore at me, Al? I'm not responsible. I'll do everything I can . . ."

The door shut off whatever else he had to say.

I forget how I spent the rest of the day, except that I walked at least five miles around downtown Los Angeles, kicking stray dogs and snarling at babies. Idaho wasn't at the hotel when I got there. She came in about five. By that time I was ready to apologize for acting like a crumb, but it wasn't necessary. She seemed to have forgotten it.

But I still wanted to make it up to her, somehow. She had never been in Los Angeles before, so that night I took her to the Sunset Strip and spent too much money. We had a good time. Everything was just the way it had been with us before the scrap. Next day I hired a car and took her on a rubberneck tour. The morning was nice, but the weather turned sour in the afternoon. We ended up at the planetarium in Griffith Park, lying back in reclining chairs watching stars swirl around overhead on what looked more like the night sky than anything I remembered seeing in Los Angeles. I felt pretty good, sitting there in the dark with Idaho's hand in mine, not thinking much, just listening to the lecturer's voice drone on while he pointed out constellations with a little arrow of light.

I was half asleep when he stopped talking for a minute. A buzz came from the big projector in the middle of the room. The stars on the dome overhead slid sideways. The Southern Cross swam up over the horizon.

The lecturer's voice said, "You are now looking at the night sky from the latitude of Santiago, Chile. It is midsummer there, midwinter in the northern hemisphere. The time is . . ."

I didn't hear what time it was. I grabbed Idaho's arm, and we stumbled over a lot of legs getting out to the aisle. It earned us several complaints, including a couple from the lecturer. The attendant at the door didn't want to open it while the lecture was going on, but it was easier to open it than put up with the row I was making. We went home.

Idaho didn't say anything about it, so I didn't either. We didn't talk at all until we got back to the hotel. There was a telephone message for her. She put the message blank on the table when we got to the room. I couldn't help seeing that she was supposed to call Mr. Devlin bright and early the next morning.

I said, "I thought you didn't know anybody in Los Angeles."

"I didn't. I do now."

I went over to the window and looked at the traffic crushing its way up Main Street.

"I've been looking for a job," Idaho said. "Mr. Devlin is personnel manager at the Security-First National Bank."

"Oh."

I went on watching the traffic.

"We have to talk about it sooner or later, Al. It might as well be now. When are you going back to Mexico?"

"Tomorrow."

"Do you want me to go with you?"

"I won't be able to pay you as big a salary as a bank."

"Never mind the salary. Do you want me to go?"

"If you want to."

"I want to. Under certain conditions."

"What conditions?"

I heard her take a breath, like a diver getting ready to jump.

"You might call them reasonable conditions of employment, or reasonable employer-employee relations. I know you've been upset about the Ruano business, and I'm not just pecking at you because of what happened the other night. It's more than that. You're not an easy person to understand. I don't know how you feel about —me. You brought me back from Chile because you felt a responsibility toward me . . ."

"More than that."

"How much more?"

I couldn't answer her.

"I'm not trying to force you into saying something you don't want to say, Al. You never made me any promises, and you don't owe me any now. But I have to know where I stand. Sometimes I think I mean something to you, and sometimes you treat me like an—an old suitcase you grab up when you want to go somewhere. If I go back to Mexico with you, how long will it last? I'd like to—be with you, but not just for a week or a month or a year. I want to work hard at anything I'm doing, so I can feel that I'm getting somewhere—that there's a future in it. It doesn't matter if it's a job at a bank or something else. I want a long-term contract. Or nothing."

She ran out of breath.

I was still watching the traffic. Automobiles and streetcars pushed their way into a tighter jam every minute, clanging their bells and blatting their horns uselessly while the traffic cop on the corner sweated to keep them moving. It was almost as bad as Mexico City, although nothing could be as bad as Mexican traffic. Mexico City was a loony bin by any standard. And yet I wanted to be back there, living my own life, doing what I wanted to do whenever I felt like it, without having to think how it might affect somebody else or fit in with somebody else's plans or wonder if it was right or wrong or good or bad in any way except as it affected me. I was tired of thinking about other people's problems. I wasn't tired of Idaho, yet. But if I took her with me, I took her problems as well—problems of How long? and How much? and How truly? even if they never got any worse. I knew the time would come when I couldn't give her the fair answer I owed her now.

I said, "There's no future for you in Mexico, Idaho."

"None at all?"

"No. I'm sorry."

Nothing happened right away. Then she came over and put her arms around me from behind.

"I'm sorry too, Al. But thanks for telling me. Now let's go out and celebrate my new job."

18

I SENT my bill off to Adams as soon as I arrived in
Mexico City. Until I got around to figuring expenses, I
had completely forgotten the twenty-five hundred
dollar credit he had sent to the bank in Santiago. It was
still there. I wrote to tell him about it, explained that it
would be impossible for me to get the money from
where I was, and suggested that he try to recover it
from his end. I would be glad to cooperate in any way
possible. Please remit as per enclosed statement, yours
very truly, A. Colby. It was strictly a business letter.

His answer, with a check, came back a couple of days
later. Clipped to his letter was a copy of another letter,
air mail, addressed to Señor Rodolfo Ruano, c/o National City Bank, Santiago, Chile, marked Urgent, Private and Confidential. Adams' letter to me said:

Dear Al—

I gather from your brief note that you are still sore
at me. I am sure that you will get over it when you have
time to think about my position. At least I sincerely
hope so.

I enclose a check in settlement of your account. Do
not worry about the money in Chile, as my bank says it

can be recovered. I also enclose a copy of a letter which I have written to Parker, taking all precautions that it will reach him and him only. The letter, I believe, speaks for itself. It was written only after a great deal of thought and considerable mental strain on my part. I am no more of a heel than is necessary in my profession.

Sincerely,
Chuck

P.S. I will keep you informed of developments in the case.

His letter to Parker was fair enough, as far as the wording went. He had leaned over backward to keep it from sounding tough. But he had laid everything on the line. A quarter of a million dollars hung on Parker's signature. Adams was willing to do everything possible to save Parker from embarrassment, but the signature would have to be given. He knew all the facts in the case, sympathized with Parker's position, and regretted that it was necessary for him to ask that Parker communicate with him with a view to making prompt arrangements. He would be glad to forward the documents to Chile or receive Parker in California, whichever Parker preferred. He would wait exactly two weeks for Parker's reply. At the end of that time, he would be regretfully obliged to request assistance from the United States Consular Service.

And may God have mercy on your soul. It wasn't in

the letter, but it should have been. Roberto Ruano Parker was as good as dead.

They were the longest two weeks I ever spent in my life. I tried playing thirty-six holes of golf every day, just to keep busy. After I wrapped a forty-dollar putter around a tree because a bird twittered at me, I gave up golf. Then a friend asked me to drive up to his *hacienda* in Fortín de las Flores. It was too quiet in Fortín for my nerves. I went on to Vera Cruz. It was too hot there, too cold in Taxco, too noisy in Monterrey, too damn much of everything everywhere else I went. I got back to Mexico City on the fourteenth day—it was Christmas Eve—and found a telegram waiting for me.

I wanted it to be Season's Greetings from somebody. I didn't care who. It wasn't. It said:

CASE CLOSED WITH PARKER'S DEATH LAST WEEK. JUST RECEIVED AUTHENTIC REPORT. SORRIER THAN I CAN SAY.
CHUCK.

The strange thing was that I felt better right away. It was the waiting that had got me, more than anything else. Now that it was over, I could stop sweating about it. But I had to know how it had happened.

I sent a cable to Lee in Valparaíso, asking him to check up on the facts. He cabled back that he was still waiting to hear my end of the story, and that don Rodolfo Ruano Parker had been shot to death by Víctor Chavarría Serra, an employee. The facts of the killing were obscure. There was a rumor that don Rodolfo had made an attempt to turn Chavarría over to the *carabineros* for a murder which had allegedly occurred four or five years before, but the authorities were puzzled by this, since they knew of no murder which fit the circumstances. However, questions of Chavarría's guilt or innocence in the matter were unimportant. He had himself been shot and killed by the *carabineros* as don Rodolfo lay dying at his feet. The law had been satisfied.

I was probably the only man alive who knew just how well the law had been satisfied. A murder had been paid for, a murderer executed, a false death made real. It was all over, for me as well as for the old man.

So I hopped a plane and went back to Chile.

I didn't know why I was going back even after I was on my way. All across the length of Central America and down that hell-burnt South American desert coastline, I kept asking myself, What are you doing this for? Why spend your own money on a useless trip? What do you expect to do after you get there? Are you crazy?

The only question I could answer was the last one. I was crazy.

The plane got into Santiago late, after dark. I went straight from the airport to the big house on Avenida O'Higgins. A wreath of black flowers hung from the knocker on the front door. The maid who answered the door was in black—black clothes, black shoes, black stockings, not a single touch of white to relieve it. She was as ugly as a lump of coal. Everybody in that house would wear the same costume for at least a year, maybe longer, because death is an ugly thing and no one must be permitted to forget its ugliness and think of the pleasures of life. Particularly the man who has caused a death, if he should happen to come calling.

I said to the maid, "Is doña María at home?"

"She does not yet receive visitors, *señor*."

"Don Fito?"

"He is not at home."

I swallowed.

"Señorita María Teresa?"

"I will tell her that you are here."

She went away.

I waited a hundred years. There wasn't a sound in the house, not even a clock ticking. It was like a tomb. I heard Terry's heels coming before I saw her. The sweat broke out on the palms of my hands.

She was in solid black, like the maid. It didn't look ugly on her. There wasn't any kind of clothing that could make her look ugly.

I didn't know what to say, because I didn't know how much she knew. I wouldn't have been surprised if she had spat at me, or turned her back, or had me thrown out of the house. Instead, she held out her hand, took mine, and let it drop quickly.

"You were good to come, Ahl. You came all the way from Mexico?"

"As soon as I heard."

We were both uncomfortable. Her eyes shifted away from mine. She said, "Come sit down."

We went into the big gloomy *sala* and sat down, three

feet apart on a sofa.

I said, "How is doña María?"

"She will be better, after a while."

"Fito?"

"He is well."

"How does he feel about what happened at the airport?"

"He is grateful that you kept him from killing you, of course."

She was as cold as one of the marble statues, on the surface. Underneath, something was stirring; fear, nervousness, hatred, maybe bottled-up grief. I didn't know what it was. But it showed in the way she kept from meeting my eye for more than a moment, and the stiff way she sat, like a good hostess entertaining a stranger at tea. She kept her hands clasped tightly together around a black handkerchief.

We were talking Spanish, a fine language for the discussion of death and betrayals and sadness. I said, "I know very little of what happened. Does it distress you to talk about it?"

"No. But I know very little myself. The *administrador* at the *fundo* killed him in a quarrel about the—the other death."

"Is it true that your father tried to turn the *administrador* over to the police?"

"I don't know. I can't believe it. Chavarría could have exposed him. I think Chavarría himself must have threatened my father, for some reason."

I thought my own thoughts. She began to roll the

black handkerchief back and forth, back and forth, between her palms.

"It was a terrible thing," I said.

"It would have been more terrible if he had died with his mind troubled about his—difficulties, instead of in peace at last. Fito and I are both very grateful for what you did, Ahl. We know what it must have cost you."

"What I did?"

"The letter you wrote him. He told us about it."

I didn't say anything. I couldn't.

"As it turned out, you didn't have to lie. The affidavits are true, now. But it was wonderful of you."

Sitting still after that was more than I could manage. I lit a cigarette and used the burnt match as an excuse to stand up and cross the room, where there was an ash tray on a table. It was the table where I had first seen the photograph of Terry as a child.

Two photographs stood on the table now, hers and Fito's. My cellophane frame for Fito's picture had been replaced by a gilt frame matching the other one. The family was safe at home.

I said, "The letter I wrote him relieved his mind, then?"

"Of course."

I thought: Wife deserter, bigamist, murderer and liar to his death. He hadn't done it to make me look good. He had done it so his family wouldn't know that he had baited Chavarría into killing him. But in doing it he had made me look like the cheat and liar he was, the cheat that Terry had tried to make me with her raspberry lipstick, the liar she must think I had been for her sake. That was why she sat there rolling the handkerchief nervously in her hands, afraid to look at me. She thought she had bought me off, and that I had come back to collect what she owed me.

I said, "Terry!"

She kept her eyes on the black handkerchief.

"Look at me, Terry. I want you to hear the truth and know it is the truth."

She began to shiver. She still wouldn't look up. I took three quick steps, seized both her hands, and yanked her to her feet, making her face me. The minute I saw her face, I knew what had pulled me back to Chile. It knocked everything I had to say out of my mind. All I had left was enough sense to reach for her.

We stood there, our arms tightly around each other, her head against my chest. It must have been five minutes before she said, "Ahl."

"Yes."

"I love you. More than my life."

"I love you, too."

"Truly?"

"Truly."

"I prayed that you would come back. And I did not know how to tell you when I saw you."

"I did not know until this minute."

"I knew when you wrote to tell my father that you would not expose him. I knew that you did it for me. That is when I loved you. But even before . . ."

She tried to lift her face. I put my hand on her molasses-taffy head and held it where it was.

After a while she said, "You will stay here in Chile, Ahl? I can not leave my mother now, and you must not go away from me."

"I will stay as long as you want me to stay."

"Forever, then."

Her arms tightened.

No, I thought. It won't be forever, nor for very long. Some day I'll have to tell you the truth. But not now. Later. Later, *querida mía*.

Acknowledgements

Bringing the *The Long Escape* back into print after an absence of over 60 years would not have been possible without the collective efforts of several highly creative people.

Randal S. Brandt is a librarian at the University of California, Berkeley. He discovered David Dodge in a hotel room in Mexico City in 1994 when he and his wife read a tattered copy of *The Long Escape* aloud together one rainy afternoon. With the assistance and encouragement of Dodge's daughter, Kendal, he created "A David Dodge Companion" (www.david-dodge.com). He also maintains "Golden Gate Mysteries" (bancroft.berkeley.edu/sfmystery), an online bibliography of crime and detective fiction set in the San Francisco Bay Area. He lives in Berkeley, California.

Gerhard Hüdepohl, a German semi-professional photographer, has lived in Chile since 1997 and frequently travels to remote places to photograph landscape, flora and fauna where nature is still untouched. Some of his favorite locations are the Atacama Desert, Antarctica and Sub-Antarctic Islands, the rainforests and glaciers of Patagonia or the jungle and mountains of Bolivia. His photos have been published and exhibited worldwide. Visit his studio at www.atacamaphoto.com.

Kendal Reynoso Lukrich is David Dodge's granddaughter and is a key supporter of our efforts to rekindle interest and enthusiasm for her grandfather's novels. Kendal lives with her family in Utah.

Michelle Policicchio is the graphics designer for Bruin Books. After seeing her stunning photograph of a common housefly, I knew I had found our new cover girl. She lives in Eugene, Oregon.

I owe a debt of thanks to everyone, but especially to Randy, whose stewardship of the Dodge legacy continues to inspire me. Randy knows more about books than anyone I've ever met. –JE